TALES OF TEDDY
and
AFTERNOON IN THE BALCONY

TALES OF TEDDY

and

AFTERNOON IN THE BALCONY

Two Novellas

by

STEVE DUNHAM

TALES OF TEDDY

SIX REMINISCENCES

I. LAURAMOR

Sitting in his glassy, art-filled house on a balmy sea isle one day, Teddy could not get his mind off another place he had known decades ago in Toledo, the Ohio metropolis where he'd been born in 1940... the last year of the beautiful LaSalle and the first of our brash modern era.

He could vividly recall it... a stark white Art Deco cube dwarfed by many of its prodigious, rambling neighbors garbed in correctly quaint period styles. It was the setting which made that faraway boxy house achingly special to Teddy, occupying as it did a choice corner of Eagle Point Colony, the most effete of several residential provinces of Toledo's highest society.

Situated across and a bit upriver from the city, Eagle Point was hard to get to... as was the entire East River Road where dwelled in their various estates the Libbeys, Fords, Knights, Dodges, Secors, Stranahans, and MacNicholses. If their tastes had been less refined and more literal, their gatehouses would have been adorned with giant glass bottles, headlights, spark plugs, and piggy banks to commemorate where their money came from.

Travelers to Eagle Point had either of two gauntlets to run, equally far depending upon where one started. Through staid and sooty old downtown... over the squat, ugly Cherry Street bridge or across the soaring, harplike Anthony Wayne bridge... past the domes of Hungarian basilicas and the crummy, asphalt-sheathed bungalows and stinky oil refineries of the city's East side... over narrow, pot-holed streets and rickety canal bridges to Rossford, a blighted agglomeration of gigantic glass factories, dying trees, and barracks-like company housing... then down an easy-to-miss, ordinary byway to the forbidding, gargoyle-encrusted stone piers guarding the entrance of the Colony.

Or you could drive out Broadway, through Toledo's decrepit, Edward Hopperish South end... past the shuttered, eerie remains of Walbridge Amusement Park where Teddy, as a little kid, threw up all over his youthful nursemaid for dragging him onto the Tilt-A-Whirl... down the svelte and shady West River

1

Road through the snooty town of Maumee, named for the river... across it and into the highly Republican village of Perrysburg, home of the exclusive Carranor Hunt and Polo Club and several descendants of Rutherford B. Hayes... back up the East River Road past all those gated estates, and thence to Eagle Point.

Young Teddy had willingly made the trip by either route countless times long ago, when the white boxy house belonged to his last-ever girlfriend, Rachel Morrissey. It was she who had summarily pushed him off into the abyss of life, as he liked to remember it. In fact she had "outed" him – at least to himself – and that was a start.

Rachel's parents, Edward and Laura, lived in the house since it was erected in 1939 as a wedding gift from Laura's well-heeled family, the Reinggelds. A couple of other, larger, Bauhaus-style Reinggeld residences nestled nearby and, though mostly hidden by towering hedges, they all seemed to thumb their noses at the picturesque but conventional architecture of Eagle Point.

Moreover, Eagle Point and the entire East River Road were sprinkled with Reinggelds and their kin: the Lambeths, Spitznaugles, and Pymlicos, all of whose financial interests were intertwined in banking, dry goods, and attorneyship. Their clannishness resulted in a whole succession of little scions christened with monikers like Spitznaugle Pymlico or Lambeth Reinggeld the Third... and nicknamed "Lambsy" or "Spitz."

Edward Morrissey was regarded as a tolerated outsider by his wife's circle. Her own sister (married to a Spitznaugle) snidely reminded Laura, over their daily cocktails, that she had wed the mere comptroller of a paper bag plant.

When Teddy knew him, Mr. Morrissey was tall but grossly overweight, his once-striking, dark good looks marred by an alcoholic's bulbous nose. He drove a battered, befinned black Chrysler, which looked forlorn and tubby when parked amidst the Reinggeld crowd's Coupe de Villes and Mercedes convertibles.

Amusing to some Eagle Pointers was Teddy's status as even more of an outsider – a mere Toledoan, though tolerated. He drove a toad-like old DeSoto, of which he was very proud because of its unblemished velour upholstery. When parked next to Teddy's car, Mr. Morrissey's looked positively sleek.

Teddy only came into Rachel's life on the rebound from her bitter affair with their older, irresistibly sexy friend, Rob Fielding. The girl was small beyond demure – shy, dark-eyed, dark-haired, even mousy. She was sheltered so by her usually inebriated, but nevertheless strict, parents that Teddy had never before laid eyes upon her among the young country club set that he frequented.

His life through high school and the beginnings of college had been focused, but questioningly, upon being a part of this set. Toledo was a notable old industrial center with a world-class art museum, a university, numerous corporate headquarters, and even an underworld which ranked with that of Chicago or Detroit. Socially the town nourished a sophisticated web of tangential circles, cultured and not-so-cultured... and Teddy, at only twenty, had immersed himself in a surprising cross-section of them, particularly a *demimonde* of night-life characters who were opening doors that he longed to venture further through... and would, as life unfolded.

There were half a dozen elite establishment clubs: the aforementioned Carranor... the idyllic park-like Sylvania... the "Babbitty" Inverness, where important golf tournaments were held... the dowagerly Country Club, its white-columned verandas and Hamptonish gray shingles ensconced across the river from Eagle Point... the smartly rustic Yacht Club... and the astoundingly baronial Toledo Club downtown. There was also a really swanky Jewish club, Glengarry – its medieval battlements frowning improbably over the bean fields far from town.

All of these were landmarks of Teddy's social venue and also that of his family, not that they were rock-solid members of any! Teddy and his younger sisters, Missy and Jayne, had spent their lives as guests of others, and he had begun to acknowledge a gnawing anxiety that such a life simply could not go on.

Their father, Dr. Marmaduke Chase, was a noted physician who, as a middle-aged widower, had married a striking, taciturn girl thirty years his junior. "Duke" and June Chase had, without any great effort, managed to provide the three children they produced with just about every advantage from their imposing but inwardly crumbling Tudor house near Kenwood Boulevard. It was situated in the tony enclave called Old Orchard, next to the sublimely exclusive village of Ottawa Hills – where Teddy and his mother wished they really lived.

Old Orchard and Ottawa Hills were places where you could walk or drive and see gauzy summer curtains, or a french door, riffled by the night wind and overhear a phonograph playing "Dancing in the Dark." Teddy's other favorite neighborhood was the Old West End... blocks and blocks of palatial but down-at-the-heels, Gilded Age edifices built by venerable "silk stocking" families, the city's original movers and shakers... now occupied mostly by queer antiques dealers or large Catholic households wishing to reside near the skirts of towering Rosary Cathedral.

Somehow floating along in this society soup, the Chases were nowhere as affluent as their many friends. Because of Dr. Chase's advancing age and waning energy – as well as his utterly non-mercenary nature – his income potential dwindled more and more, slowly but surely. Teddy and his sisters endured years of bitter parental quarrels over money.

Club dues, charitable responsibilities, domestic help, new cars, catered parties, summers at Michigan lakes or Virginia Beach – all had their heyday, then slipped silently over the side of the listing family ship. Teddy's own couple of years at a famously top-drawer, but crushingly expensive, all-male college in the Ohio hill country were made possible only with ungrudging but halfhearted sacrifices by his father, a personal loan by his River Road godparents, and his mother's reluctant and unhappy return to work as a hospital nurse – something Dr. Chase had rescued her from when they married.

Now back home from the school which his family could no longer afford, Teddy was missing it terrifically, especially his friendships with youths whose families owned summer places on Long Island, or who invited him to stay in Park Avenue duplexes and date girls from Darien or Scarsdale. His forays into New York (once he and a classmate drove back to Ohio in a battered MG with barely the gas money between them) were dreams come true... dreams evoked by his boyhood readings of

4

Marquand, Fitzgerald, O'Hara, and Salinger. He cherished the gem-like vignettes which now began happening to him... a solitary lunch surrounded by discreetly leering, handsome young men in the Plaza's Oak Room (lamb chop with little ruffled pants and a martini, six bucks plus tip) ... a fuzzy late night with a warm, approachable guy at the bar of the Village Vanguard... had they "made it" or hadn't they? He'd blanked that episode out.

At an early age Teddy truly believed that he had mastered the ropes of the smart set by virtually memorizing the witticisms of Nancy Mitford, Noel Coward, Somerset Maugham, and Evelyn Waugh, not to mention the edicts set forth in his mother's decorating book by Dorothy Draper... *"If you have any stained glass, be ruthless and get rid of it!"*

Here in Toledo, limbo-like, watching most of his old chums, school dates, and party hosts launch themselves – or more likely be launched by "daddy" – into responsible adult pursuits, he became morosely drawn into exploring that one last untapped societal bastion, Eagle Point.

Enter Miss Rachel Morrissey, whom Teddy had somehow missed among all the riding lessons, ballroom classes, butler-served dinners, and coming-out dances. Their parents didn't know each other either... *"What good're doctors-s-sh?",* a tipsy Laura Morrissey would quip, *"They just s-s-shpoil all yer fun."* Any peers Teddy knew had who had ever mentioned Rachel dismissed her as a wallflower. Their brief, fateful friendship came about through a back door...

Teddy was spending his first summer and fall out of college working downtown, high up in the Streamline Moderne Ohio Citizens Trust tower, for the stuffy law firm of Buller, Barrington, Feeny and Dodge as a messenger, library shelver, and general "Boy Friday." He loved the building's dazzling Byzantine lobby of pure travertine, the bustling, cacophonous canyons of old downtown Toledo, and the law office itself with its softly-lit, leather-laden atmosphere redolent of pipe smoke and furniture polish. For a time he actually enjoyed his servile role, kowtowing to the fusty old partners and joshing gamely with the younger ones and the office girls. But he became bored and just knew it could not go on.

Though he could ill afford it, Teddy liked a martini and club sandwich at The Swivel Chair, a fancy men-only noontime watering hole. In fact, when an Ottawa Hills surgeon and old family friend invited Teddy there that summer for a "man-to-man lunch" – to see if his guest had any romantic intentions regarding his debutante daughter (he did not) – the doctor was somewhat appalled to discover that such a young fellow was not only a regular patron but would order more than one martini if given the chance. Affordable or not, The Swivel Chair's ambiance and clientele appealed to Teddy infinitely more than that of the White Tower hamburger joint down the street.

At The Swivel Chair one afternoon, Teddy purposely sought out and conversed seriously for the first time with the smooth-mannered, handsome Rob Fielding – a divorced ex-Marine and the manager of another of Teddy's barely affordable haunts, a tiny but pricey men's clothier around the corner called Old Lyme. Standoffish in its studied gentlemen's pub decor, the place purveyed such classy items as Gant and Sero shirts, Harris tweed jackets, Southwick suits, and Burberry rainwear. A few seasons back the store had offered beautifully refurbished 1920's raccoon coats for a princely hundred dollars, and Teddy was one of the handful of patrons who actually bought one, bravely wearing it everywhere without feeling silly.

Old Lyme was operated by a dissolute bachelor uncle of Rachel Morrissey's, Maurice Pymlico, who was insufferably snobbish, wickedly witty, and – it was snickeringly believed by many – had designs on his lithe, green-eyed employee Rob. Teddy also had designs on Rob but didn't know how to be the aggressor, his whole sexual life preferring to be the one seduced.

Maurice also ran Old Lyme shops, and had living quarters, in Sarasota and East Hampton, and he flitted from one to another upon seasonal whim, sometimes taking Rob with him.

The Swivel Chair lunch with Rob brought about Teddy's resignation from the law firm, where he was sincerely missed, and his employment as a more-than-fulltime salesman at Old Lyme. He took to it ecstatically, spending almost all his waking hours in the company of the charismatic Rob and two other hunky, good-natured college-boy clerks, Tom and Dan.

Maurice kept a coy distance from all of them except Rob, so Teddy looked especially forward to his rare appearances at the shop or at lunch with their whole group in the dark, noisy Madison Buffet next door. Maurice was a balding, but strikingly distinguished, man of forty or so, with limpid, glittering black eyes and a permanent, intimidating smirk on his face. Always nattily dressed, he drove an Antediluvian silver Jaguar and lived in a little guest house on one of the Reinggeld's estates.

It was they – and his cousins the Lambeths – who actually owned Old Lyme and who were none too pleased with Maurice's cavalier *modus operandi.* He usually exuded a slight reek of martinis, along with Canoe and other men's fragrances the store carried. Teddy remembered reading somewhere that *"A gentleman never wears cologne"* but smugly kept it to himself.

Still, Maurice's family connections, seeming ease of life, biting *repartee,* and off-color reputation were utterly fascinating to Teddy. He was everything Teddy then wished he might like to become – enough so that, years later, upon the chance reading of his onetime mentor's obituary, Teddy sent a tribute to Williams College, Maurice's alma mater.

On days that Maurice did occasionally preside at Old Lyme, he often carried out a cruel but amusing routine when dealing with browsers, or even customers, who seemed too bumptious to gain his serious interest. He treated such persons with outrageous obsequiousness, a parody of Bertie Wooster's Jeeves punctuated *ad nauseam* with a lot of "Would the *Gentleman* care to..." and "Very good, Sir!" He also encouraged Rob, Teddy, and the others to follow suit and, watching one another's performance pokerfaced, they would later mercilessly critique each other's "Very good, Sirs." Maurice also maintained a little recipe box of file cards on all his charge-account patrons with cryptic comments scribbled on many, such as: "Deadbeat," "Klepto," "Kike," "Uppity Nigger," "Fag." Rob knew these cards by heart, but enjoyed showing them to a scandalized Teddy – who once checked on his own and found no notation.

7

Teddy's infatuation with Rob drew him into a new milieu – that of the city's many nightclubs and cocktail bars... from the ritzy Park Lane, to the gangstery Kin Wa Low's, to the black-and-tan dives of Indiana Avenue. There were also half a dozen sleazy gay bars, which Rob could tantalizingly describe but which Teddy did not have the nerve to enter.

With all this came double dates with older, often divorced, girls who worked in banks, insurance offices, or lounges. One was a psychologist named Felice who played the french horn in the Toledo Symphony. A tall, almost Amazonian brunette, she would swoop into the Towne Club or other agreed-upon meeting place after a concert, dragging her encased horn with her as casually as a purse, plunk it down with a loud guffaw, and order a Black Russian or a vodka neat.

Once when Xavier Cugat's orchestra was playing the shimmering dark blue Shalimar Room, Teddy danced with the band's slinky blonde singer between every set. These girls all thought Teddy was sweet and precocious for his age, Rob's cute young sidekick – a refreshing change from the hardened males they had misspent much time with. And he was relieved that not much was expected of him by them.

Through the doting Maurice, Rob had been long involved with Maurice's niece Rachel, and Teddy often found himself a third wheel on some of their evenings together. Even though Rachel's parents were virtual alcoholics themselves – or, no doubt, because of this – they hotly disapproved of Rob's behavior (he held prodigious amounts of liquor, until it was too late) and they managed to influence Rachel, one night, to kick Rob out the front door for good.

Soon afterward, Rachel phoned Teddy and asked him to escort her to a Maumee Valley Country Day School alumni dinner dance, thereby becoming Teddy's last-ever girlfriend.

Maumee Valley was the private school which nearly all River Road and Eagle Point kids attended, unless they were sent away to boarding schools. Those going to public school usually had been kicked out of Maumee Valley, or some august institution in the East, or both. But Teddy's father believed fiercely in the excellence and egalitarianism of public schools (despite his own Ivy League degree), so that's where Teddy went until his disastrous college caper. Perhaps that's why he was invariably flattered by attention from most any private-schooler that he ever met.

At first Teddy tried very hard to like, but could barely stomach, the outwardly prim, intense Rachel. He actually became very much more fond of Edward and Laura, despite their sometimes rotten dispositions. Mrs. Morrissey was a goggle-eyed, wizened little imp somewhat resembling Imogene Coca, yet Teddy found her presence in a room more arresting than that of his own mother. Her husband was a great bear of a man totally preponderated by the two diminutive females in his lair.

Above all Teddy loved driving along the winding lanes of Eagle Point, a privileged guest, until he reached a certain one... guarded by a phalanx of Reinggeld hedges and paved in evocative, squishy little seashells. It led to the glass-block entry of Rachel's white box with its urbane corner windows, vaguely nautical decks and railings, and lush lawn leading down to the river. The smell of new-mown grass, the wink of lightning bugs, and the late summer sirens of locusts would always bring him back to this spot.

Inside, near the stairway which swept sinuously up past a moon-shaped window, you'd suddenly and raucously be greeted by the Morrissey's pack of lovable but unkempt dogs; barking madly, slobbering, their coats tangled and filthy. Their nails scratched and their loose hairs littered the dusty parquet floors. One little spaniel always made Teddy wince when he had to look at its missing left eye, like a popped button on a stuffed animal.

The furniture in the french-doored living and dining rooms reminded Teddy of exactly the kind donated to the Little Theater, as props for its English drawing-room comedies. Good, but old and nicked-up.

Over the fireplace hung a stunning, gold-framed, full-length portrait of Laura Morrissey at the time of her marriage. Sylph-like yet commanding, capped with a whimsical mop of marcelled hair, she bore no resemblance to Imogene Coca. Below the picture, boldly carved into the stone hearth was an inscription:

9

L A U R A M 0 R. It was the name Edward's father-in-law had given the house, as a reminder of who had paid for it.

Mindful of the inexorable pain which that inscription must have fomented over the years, Teddy loved it, found it irresistibly poignant, and would stare at it and the picture for long moments whenever he could. Exactly like the example of Proust's evanescent *madeleine* floating in a cup of tea, or the du Maurier character Rebecca's contemplation of the ruined manor above the cliffs of Cornwall, a recurring image of that gracefully incised mantel could conjure up Teddy's entire disquieted youth in an instant.

Most of Teddy and Rachel's evenings were spent in Lauramor's dusty-floored living room, simply talking over books or movies they knew about and playing cards or badgammon. Rachel drank very little, for she thoroughly abhorred her parents's affliction – but she generously served their liquor to Rob and, later, to Teddy. The Morrisseys liked Teddy because he was restrained, like Rachel, but unlike her seemed to hang onto their every word.

The beginning of the end came one week with the arrivals at Old Lyme of truck upon truck of unsold merchandise from Maurice's two out-of-state shops, including crates and crates of hideous but very costly Paisley neckties which nobody would buy. The Reinggeld and Lambeth bean counters had finally pulled the plug on Maurice's follies in the clothing trade.

Rob must have had some warning, but did not tell Teddy, Tom, and Dan until the first van pulled up that Old Lyme was going out of business. Their jobs would be to change the price tags on all the new items, marking them up as much as twice – then marking them down in bold red ink to a "bargain" price. Store hours, for the first time, were extended into the evening and also to Sunday afternoons. Despite the doomsday atmosphere – *Last Day of Sale New Year's Eve!* – Teddy so relished this behind-the-scenes experience in retail strategy, and spent so much time in the shop, that his overtime wages alone well might have hastened the bankruptcy.

Maurice Pymlico hardly darkened the door anymore, and hordes of buyers – bumptious and otherwise – poured in so fast day after day that there was no more time for, "Very good, Sir!" A hardworking but simple girl named Effie was hired to tally sales slips and gift wrap parcels. She couldn't spell, thereby producing such momentarily puzzling receipts as: *3 scrafs, 2 shits.*

Old Lyme's demise must have jinxed the entire 200 block of North Erie Street, once the Rodeo Drive, or Fifth Avenue, of downtown Toledo. Next sank the Tiffany-like six-story Van Ardsdahl jewelers, the elegant Lambeth Brothers department store, The Swivel Chair, and the cushy Rattner fur salon, outside which many a matron's limousine waited without fear of a parking ticket. All of these venerable enterprises dried up or moved to suburban malls, leaving a vista of naked, staring show windows and riven awnings.

Most jarring was the utter implosion of Old Lyme's next-door neighbor, the city's revered old brokerage house, Pfell and Heckwith. Unbeknown to its blue-blooded clients, the overextended firm had actually come to be controlled by a slippery pair of New Jersey financiers named Schlossberg, who one day stuffed all available cash and negotiables into their Gucci luggage and absconded for Acapulco – making Pfell and Heckwith a household word on Wall Street, and the nationwide nightly news, for at least a week. Teddy was galaxies away from home by the time all of these things happened, but he had unwittingly participated in hewing the first crack into 200 North Erie's glossy marble facade.

Teddy did not honestly know how much – if any – graphic sex had occurred between Rachel and Rob, but one glum winter day after Old Lyme closed for good and after months of never being touched by Teddy, Rachel suddenly bristled: "You've got to go away from here ... get away from everybody you know, jump off into the world! Go where there must be a lot of *Robs* for you to experiment with, where you can... be yourself!"

Teddy realized this, but had needed a provocative shove from someone whom he respected, as he now did the clairvoyant, not-so-mousy Rachel. Despite all the innuendoes about Maurice and Rob, Teddy never had the guts to hit on his idol – but instead had begun hunting encounters with other males in the after-dark world which Rob had intimated lay out there for him. How did Rachel fathom all of this? Maybe the idol had told her...

Then some final blows: Rob simply left town, without good-byes, to live with Maurice in Sarasota. Soon afterward, according to impeccable sources: Rob severely beat up Maurice, then rejoined the Marines and shipped out for Vietnam... from which he has never returned.

Meanwhile, faced with a notice that his own college-deferred draft status had expired, Teddy volunteered so that he could choose his own fate – army information school. He endured a three-year enlistment which took him far and wide, riding mercurial highs and lows of achievement, morale, and such libidinal adventures as Rachel would never have fathomed... "experiments" with wonderful guys and with some insufferable rats!

But he emerged unscathed, with letters of commendation, just before the major Asian onslaught and found himself, fancy free, an employable and reasonably talented newspaper reporter. He dived deeply into the life he wanted in provocative, stimulating cities like Atlanta, Miami, Dallas, and Chicago. He graduated, with help from the G.I. bill, from a prestigious university and by his late twenties had elevated himself to the ivory towers of magazine editing.

Best of all, Teddy found his inseparable life's companion and lover – with whom he has gleefully traveled the world and lived at very good addresses, including the palmy one from whence this chronicle began. From the day that Rachel watched him board the train for boot camp, Teddy could virtually sweep those halcyon memories of country clubs and fledgling nightlife into the toy box where they belonged.

Occasionally the prodigal son returns... to the downtown that once seemed so vibrant, now obscured behind bland new curtain walls sutured onto old, ornately crafted masonry or beneath oil-splotched parking lots and bleak plazas named for nobody he ever heard of... to his cherished Old Orchard and Ottawa Hills, where his mother now lives in a tiny apartment. When he glances over the morning newspaper's society page, the names and photos are all but unrecognizable. Nary a Reinggeld, Lambeth, or Spitznaugle – and not many others whom the Chases knew. Who could all these frozen-faced new people be, issuing invitations to cocktails by the pool or to black-tie dinner parties up and down the East and West River Road?

Teddy has never been back to Lauramor, even if he thought he could find it. The roads to Eagle Point are surely just as roundabout and torturous as they were when he was twenty... and despite the lure of locusts and fireflies, the smell of new-mown lawns descending to the river, he doesn't want to know who lives there.

*   *   *

II. THE FRENCH ROOM

When Teddy was little, he loved his mother madly. She was his best pal.

Though pampered by a succession of good-humored black domestics and indulged sometimes by his stern middle-aged father, Teddy stuck to his beautiful young mother like glue. She reminded him of June Allyson most of the time, but in moments of terrible fury she could be Barbara Stanwyck. His dad looked, and acted, like Mr. Conklin in "Our Miss Brooks." Teddy always said he'd like Betty Hutton for a babysitter, instead of crotchety old Mrs. Bowman.

The Chases first lived on a pleasantly curving, shady street on a bluff overlooking Jermain Park, a vast mysterious marshy bowl where kids were forbidden to tread (although older ones did), even in daylight. Site of a sleazy, long-vanished amusement park, its only landmark was the ruin of a murky millpond choked with cattails, into which protruded an enticing round pavilion under which, it was warned, nosy children were drowned and snakes or bogeymen lurked. Jermain Park was the only threatening presence in Teddy's early life, aside from the acerbity of his father.

During these years the household had only one car, which Dr. Chase needed much of the time, so his spouse depended on taxis or friends picking her up for her considerable social outings. Teddy was always morose and tearful at the advent of any of his mother's absences, even to visit her best friend Shirley, another doctor's wife who lived just a few houses away. But every so often, and always at Christmastime, she would put on her best June Allyson smile and take him downtown shopping and to a wondrous place for lunch.

They would walk together along their curvy shady street, then cross the wide, also forbidden, brick-paved avenue that lead to the city center and wait for the growl and rattle of an orange-and-cream monster of a bus to swallow them up and slowly convey them to a pulse-quickening world of denser and denser, taller and taller, heavily-corniced buildings which formed deafening, soot-darkened canyons of brick and terra cotta encrusted with gargoyles, turrets, and tiers of glinting, old-fashioned bay windows.

Among primeval forests of granite columns ranged honking vans, clanging streetcars, gust-driven gum and cigar wrappers, and hurtling mobs of be-hatted and gloved women like Teddy's mom scurrying every which way.

When lunchtime came, the two would negotiate the voracious, ankle-nipping revolving doors of Lasalle's, Toledo's biggest department store, and squeeze into one of a twinkling, tinkling row of mahogany-panelled, oval-domed elevators, always commanded by a person dressed like an organ grinder's monkey. Squeezing out on the seventh floor, they would turn right and enter a hushed, heavily-scented grotto, the vestibule of Lasalle's splendid dining spot – the French Room.

After getting accustomed to the seductive lighting, they would ascend a fantastically filigreed, loop-de-looping bronze staircase to the restaurant level – Teddy scrambling up one way, his mother gliding up the other – until they met at the top, laughed, and gazed upon the French Room itself. Lofty and lozenge-shaped, approached gracefully down a couple of broad, dais-like platforms, the space was clad in vivid green marble and black obsidian, subtly illumined from exquisitely wrought silvery urns, carpeted and upholstered in the softest rose, and staffed by droves of waitresses costumed as French maids. The scene later reminded Teddy of illustrations he'd seen of the ocean liner *Normandie.*

The clientele was always the same... the store's better-dressed women shoppers, their occasional escorts or offspring (usually girls), and the better-dressed store executives... in other words, very few men. But this didn't bother Teddy. He couldn't help but be fascinated by the female *milieu,* something he would learn to suppress as he grew older.

A droll children's menu touted such dishes as Humpty-Dumpty's Omelet, Chicken Little *a' la* King, and, at the very bottom, a simple dessert which Teddy found irresistible, Mr. Clown. It was only a scoop of vanilla ice cream plopped on a frilly collar-like doily, embellished with two beady little raisin

16

eyes, a snippet of maraschino for the mouth, and an upside-down waffle cone for a cap. The adult menu wasn't French at all, but the diners made do with martinis and elaborate salads. After lunch, the exhausted pair usually took a taxi home.

This routine was repeated countless times, and Teddy never tired of it. To him the French Room was at the opposite end of the earth from the dank horrors of Jermain Park. The only negative comment he ever heard about his favorite place came from his prim, bespectacled Aunt Bess who was once dutifully treated to lunch there while visiting from Kentucky. Oblivious to the ethereal decor and swanky bill of fare, the old lady would only mutter: "Hmph! Never saw so many idle women, drinking liquor and going bareheaded!"

It was 1946, and younger women were indeed beginning to shed the silly chapeaus, veils, gloves, and girdles of the pre-war world. Also that year Teddy's father obtained for his wife, through his connections as a physician, a spiffy black convertible with red leatherette and a pearly Deluxe steering wheel, one of the very few new autos available in all of Ohio so soon after V-J Day.

This gift changed everything – freed Teddy's mother to roam at will and even affected the sojourns downtown. No more buses or cabs – she now drove her car down there and parked it in the Willard Hotel garage.

Often Teddy, his mother, and new sister Missy widened their gustatory explorations to exotic new venues like Miller's Cafeteria, with its fairy-tale murals of lords and ladies, knights and castles... or the noisy but divinely pungent coffee shop sequestered behind the notions department at Lambeth Brothers, Lasalle's arch-rival... or the richly wainscoted, diamond-paned Elizabethan Room of the Willard itself. Sometimes they'd go to the chic, loungy Tick-Tock – not really a place for children – where Mrs. Chase would bemusedly spot male acquaintances meeting their mistresses in cushy booths... or to the more dignified Dyer's, redolent of starched linen and glimmering lobster tanks, where the same fellows met their wives.

In summer they breezed way out, past woods and polo fields, to Sylvania Golf Club for a swim in its cerulean pool and a bite

17

of lunch on the grotto-like screened porch... or, top down, they devoured grilled wieners and chocolate dopes at the roadside Frozen Custard, under the gaze of four fierce plaster polar bears.

One noontime Teddy walked home from school for his Campbell's soup and grilled cheese sandwich, prepared by his favorite housemaid, Isola, who was strangely quiet. Before heading back he went upstairs to the bathroom and found his mother, in a new white suit dotted with red cherries, sobbing on the maple spool bed in his room.

"Mama, I thought you were going away for lunch!"

"I was..." she sniffled.

"With Shirley? To the French Room?"

"No, honey. With Shirley's husband, Uncle Ned... to the French Room and then a musty little closet at the Willard... I went all the way up there and waited forever, at the table, for Ned; then I drove the heck back home before he showed up!" she blubbered.

The devastating honesty of this revelation was not lost on Teddy. He knew that something was wrong about it, that his mother was distraught, and that he ought never mention this day to Daddy – and he never did mention it again to his mother. Decades after the good doctor was dead, she herself confessed the escapade – jokingly, forthrightly, and with relief – at a family party.

One day in the early Fifties, after Teddy's family had moved to Old Orchard, Lasalle's closed the French Room and sealed it off for storage space. They opened a new restaurant on a lower floor called the Kountry Kitchen... cramped, garishly lighted, and festooned with fake clapboarding, gingham oilcloths on picnic benches, old iron skillets nailed to the walls and – worst of all – an ordering counter.

The menu featured burgers, "Tomato Surprise," and other quickly gobbled items. No martinis, Humpty-Dumpty, or fancy service. All of that disappeared with the advent of the hatless women and other suburbanizing of America, Teddy supposed. He likened it to television's dumbing-down of the "I Love Lucy" set from the familiar urbane Manhattan apartment to the kitschy

Connecticut ranch house – a set which very much resembled the Kountry Kitchen.

In another few years the New York owners of Lasalle's decided to close the entire store, leaving its block-square Italian Renaissance hulk to molder amid an increasingly empty downtown. Soon also standing derelict were Lambeth Brothers, the Willard, and blocks of gorgeous movie theaters... Valentine, Paramount, Rivoli, Palace, Princess. Wrecking balls vaporized most of them into naked parking lots, while mall after mini-mall marched across the cornfields toward Michigan, Indiana, or the boggy shores of Lake Erie.

Lasalle's handsome shell is still there, but recently gutted and diced up into yuppie lofts. Long grown up and living far away, Teddy read a newspaper feature by an enthusiastic but obviously ignorant young reporter, gushing over the imperfectly remembered magnificence of old Lasalle's... the shimmering, evergreen-scented holiday adornments... the forlornness of those tattered, cavernous interiors... and on and on. Nothing about the French Room!

Shocked, Teddy penned a highly descriptive missive to the editors – only to receive his letter back with a request to drastically trim it for length. He did, right into the wastebasket.

But he knows that way up in that handsome pile, in a nautilus-like chamber crammed with old dress dummies, is the ghost of his beautiful French Room. Perhaps the demolition guys, or the renovators, glimpsed it briefly and admired the lustrous green marble and curling bronze stairs... or discovered a cache of dusty little menus offering that saucy ice-cream clown... or maybe one of them stepped on Teddy's mother's red cherry brooch which had accidentally slid down between the cushions of a rose banquette, one unmentionable day.

*   *   *

III. SEMPER PARATI

Pressures that propelled twenty-year-old Teddy Chase to ditch his life in stolid Toledo were rooted in some indelibly suggestive memories of time spent, several weather bands to the south, in and around his mother's hometown of Louisville, Kentucky. Affirmation of his feelings about two elemental facets of human existence – conformity and sex – had first crept up on him while there, like the sudden overflowing of an unattended bathtub.

Even as a toddler Teddy had a vivid consciousness of Louisville, recalling overnight train trips there with Mom to visit her family. The litany began with packing up suitcases sometime after dark... then his father driving them down to Toledo's soot-blackened, turreted old Union Station amid the hubbub of taxis, porters, and gigantic steam engines chuffing impatiently to be off. Pummeled all night by clanging bells and jolting rail junctions, they would curl up and try to doze in their odd-smelling, plush-upholstered Pullman drawing room with the disappearing bunks and shiny steel toilet. Sometimes Teddy's baby sister, Missy, would be with them, commanding enough of her mother's attention that her brother could explore the dim, jostling corridors or, too excited to sleep, gaze out at the moonlit, neon-pocked townscapes. As the Ohio River flew by they would breakfast in the white-clothed dining car, served by white-coated, white-teethed Negro waiters... then shortly step down, miraculously, three hundred miles from home in Louisville.

Next came effusive greetings by Aunt Silvia, who fetched them from the depot in her navy blue '36 Ford with the outmoded floor gearshift and saucy "V-8" embossed onto the black horn button. Teddy adored older cars. His father's automobiles were always new and chromy.

Silvia and her hen-pecked accountant-husband Uncle Throckmorton, who resembled a frog with a necktie, changed domiciles rather often – too often, scoffed Teddy's father. But they always resided in the same sort of refined, rose-brick Georgian bungalow that predominated in their chosen section of the city, Saint Matthews. April was Teddy's favorite month to visit, because spring arrived in Louisville several weeks before it came to Toledo. The blinding yellow sprays of forsythia lining the streets and lanes of Saint Matthews were an intoxicating sight, an unexpected banishment of winter.

By the time he was nine or ten, Teddy's entire family – even his busy physician father – would embark on motor trips to Louisville, whizzing south through the flat, spottily forested Ohio farmland... past the puzzlingly similar, false-fronted Main Streets of Bowling Green, Findlay, and Wapakoneta, bypassing smoky old Lima – made so by the huge locomotive works there – on through the endless dun-colored city of Dayton... and out past its soaring, Buck Rogers-like Wright Brothers Memorial into the beginnings of rolling hill country. Starved for lunch, they would find refuge from the highway among the fragrant coffee urns and clattering crockery of the Canary Cottage Grille, a favorite spot along Cincinnati's Reading Road.

Fortified for the long afternoon, they would hurl on down that winding thoroughfare, deeper and deeper into the bowels of the Queen City... past monstrous factories, frowning old mansions, high-walled convents – or were they prisons? – then beneath the dingy, lace-curtained windows of decrepit, steep-roofed rowhouses marching up and down the precipitous streets, looming crazily as though poised to collapse on the Chase's big black Pontiac.

Cincinnati sometimes could be so hot and humid, its dense masonry infrastructure acting like an oven, that the entire human zoo was on display to motorists passing by. Sprawled on every stoop, drooping over every sill, were shirtless men, scraggily-haired women, or bleary dogs, cats, and kids of all colors. Bottoming out in the dark pit of downtown, they would purr into the sunlight across the ancient Roebling suspension bridge into Kentucky and upward through the town of Covington, past its also-tottering rowhouses and the famous White Horse Tavern.

Teddy, Missy, and their new sister, Jayne, would exasperate their parents by endlessly singing, "She'll Be Comin' Round the Mountain," or gravely intoning the doggerel on each cluster of Burma Shave signs, or gasping in horror at every treacherous curve, jagged limestone bluff, or hillbilly hovel along the last ninety miles of Old River Road, until finally they reached the civilized venue of Saint Matthews. Heralded by a comforting crunch of the smooth, pastel-colored pebbles in Aunt Silvia's driveway, they'd arrive just in time for supper.

Teddy couldn't remember anything about the railroad journeys home, but on some of the return auto trips he recalled stopping at a stuffy old inn called the Golden Lamb. Ever after, mirthfully – and mercilessly – his mother would remind him of their first time there... when the waitress appeared and a certain precocious little boy piped up, brightly: "I don't need a menu! I'll have some of the Golden Lamb."

His most life-shaping Kentucky experience came during the summer he was fifteen, while on a side visit to his Cousin Belinda, also fifteen but a whopping head taller and aggressively mature. Well developed and powerful for a girl, she was nevertheless cloyingly feminine – despite a slight mustache which made Teddy queasy. Belinda smothered her comparatively diminutive cousin with adoration and flattery, always hugging him and gushing loudly to everyone, in her honey-chile drawl, that she *"could just eat him up!"*

After a flurry of letters back and forth, the citified Teddy reluctantly agreed that on the family's upcoming Kentucky jaunt he would spend a weekend with Belinda, who lived with her widowed grandmother on a tobacco farm, way out in the country from Louisville near a town called Waddy.

Upon arrival Teddy was utterly shocked, not that he had expected "Tara." He truly felt sick to his stomach for the first few minutes, that Saturday morning when he first saw the ruinous place and watched the dusty retreat of the blue Ford – not to return until Sunday afternoon, eons away. His normally possessive mother could not stand Belinda's dour, inhospitable grandma, so she and Silvia came and went – affably but quickly.

Belinda's parents were divorced alcoholics, deemed unfit to raise her by the judge who had placed her on the farm. Her father's various military pensions were garnisheed to help support his daughter who, on a scholarship also finagled by the judge, was enrolled in a secluded girl's academy far away –

something that no doubt contributed to Belinda's pent-up summertime boisterousness.

The original old mansarded farmhouse had burned down a few years ago and had been replaced by a plain unpainted tract house with the same amenities as the old place – bare light bulbs in the ceiling, a bottled-gas stove, and no plumbing. Eggy well-water spluttered from the kitchen pump and a rank, lopsided privy hunkered in the backyard – way too close to the house, Teddy thought. Worse, the rear stoop and entire yard were encrusted with chicken shit, thanks to the open-door policy at the hen house.

Belinda delightedly showed her cousin around all these wonders as if they were the domain of a princess, and her contagious good spirits gradually relaxed him into looking forward to an interesting – or even good – time.

Next thing, she backed out her grandma's old Chevy: "Let's go see the Hester twins, Billy and Bobby. They're *eighteen*... I showed 'em your picture and they're nutty to meet you!"

"We don't have driver's licenses yet," admonished practical Teddy.

"We don't need 'em in the country, silly. All of us kids tool around," replied Belinda smugly, backing straight into her grandmother's mailbox..."Oh, crap!"

Laughing, they rattled off along a winding road nearly camouflaged by billowing blankets of black-eyed Susans and Queen Anne's lace, to an isolated farmstead... then way on back to a massive red barn, its fortress-like portal open just a slit.

"The boys are always in here, doin' darn knows what," explained Belinda, dragging Teddy into the pitch-dark, sweet-smelling inner sanctum.

Two perfectly formed, black-haired Adonises stepped out of the gloom, greeting Teddy with dazzling grins and firm sweaty handshakes. Barefoot and bare-torsoed, wearing only skintight jeans, the twins appeared to Teddy almost identical, but not exactly. Their facial features – chin, jaw, nose, brow – were composed in nearly the same pleasing combination, but not really. One youth's eyes, startling blue like his brother's, were hashed with traces of gold. Teddy was never sure which was Billy and which was Bobby.

Belinda made the introductions, embarrassing Teddy by calling him her "uppity Yankee cousin," and chattered on about some catty girl whom the twins and she both knew. Then she suddenly excused herself, saying that she had things to do in town and would drop back for Teddy in a bit. Off she sped, scattering the gravel, leaving her cousin with his frisky inquisitors.

Friendly, but somehow threatening, they grilled him nonstop about numerous aspects of life "up Nawth"... popular music, school sports, drag racing, liquor, girls... but nary a question about Teddy's own myriad – but to them prudish and unathletic – interests. Unsettled as some of their profane banter made him, Teddy was electrically attracted to the Hester boys – more than to anyone he had ever met. For the first time in his life, he truly welcomed a stupendous urge for *sex* that he just knew would boil over soon... and not in the tame way it always had with certain boys at home, or even sometimes with girls.

Brashly one twin (the one with gold-flecked eyes) slid his arm around Teddy's waist and entreated, "C'mon, cuz... show us what you got in them shorts."

Ecstatic but flustered, Teddy squirmed away and sank back in the straw, laughing but without a quip or excuse. Unasked, he did pull off his polo shirt. Laughing also, the twins now offered to show their guest what country boys liked to do...

Standing right above him, they peeled open their jeans and out popped their identical red-hot hard-ons. Slobbering on their fingers, both began jacking off – slowly, sensuously, stroking themselves for what seemed like forever. Then one twin slid down and began licking the other's stiff rubbery cock and playing with his furry balls. Precious time passed as his partner returned the favor and Teddy, watching raptly, rose to his knees and unfastened his own belt. Next the brothers clasped their muscled arms around each other and – slick and perspiring, belly to belly – rubbed up and down, kissing each other's neck, until the inevitable mess!

Still a little breathless, they kicked off their pants entirely and lunged, puma-like, toward Teddy: "Allright, cuz, it's yo turn..."

Suddenly out in the gravel – *scrunch!* Before Belinda could bound through the door, Billy and Bobby hopped back into their jeans and, heart sinking, Teddy scrambled into his shirt as the Hesters enthusiastically told her, "We was showin' your cuz how we wrassle."

"You imps! Well, I'm kidnapping him and taking him to the ice cream social in Waddy tonight. Got him a date with Carole Sue, too. How 'bout *that?*"

Groaning simultaneously, the Hesters grinned slyly at Teddy, politely bid him good-bye with especially sticky handclasps – and hoped he'd surely come back sometime.

Not knowing – then – that he'd never see them again, Teddy euphorically endured the rest of his visit, beginning with the greasy supper grudgingly prepared by Belinda's grandmother. Afterward he waited on the back stoop among the smelly chickens, while Belinda sponged off in a galvanized tub set up in the kitchen and laced with water heated on the stove.

Thanks to his cousin's too-short shopping spree, Teddy thought glumly, he hadn't done anything that day to warrant taking a bath!

He tolerated Carole Sue (who had a screechy laugh and pointy glasses) and the small-town social – and later sleeping upstairs in a stifling, sparsely furnished room where bugs flew in and out all night through screenless dormers. It contained one intriguing piece, a battered old Eastlake loveseat, the only surviving artifact from the burned farmhouse.

Things like that tantalized Teddy, but not as much as his afternoon with the Hester boys.

In the autumn of the following year, after school had started, he was granted a week off to accompany his mother to Louisville on family business. By then he was sixteen, the proud and eager possessor of a driver's license, helping to chauffeur Mom down there in her new little white Italian convertible.

They wouldn't be seeing Belinda, who was already shipped across the state to school, but a few doors down the street from

Silvia's house was the residence of her longtime church friends, the Hatchers. Teddy and his family were, at best, nominal Episcopalians... but their aunt and uncle and most of the Hatchers (mother, father, and mildly retarded older son, John) were fundamentalist followers of the Bible... "Disgustingly churchy," Teddy called them, for they hurried off to their little wooden gothic sanctuary on Highland Avenue for hours every Sunday, morning and night, and some week nights as well.

However, John's younger brother Jeff, who Teddy had known slightly all his life, was now a strapping fifteen-year-old – and not a bit religious when out of sight from home.

Wiry but firmly muscled, already a varsity football player at the local high school, Jeff carried himself with a certain insouciance, very like that briefly glimpsed a summer ago in the Hester twins. Otherwise he didn't resemble them; he was taller, yet sort of puppy-like, with a frizzled brush cut and alert, dark brown eyes. He and his gregarious, endomorphic buddies, many of whom attended the city's exclusive Country Day School, all dressed very much alike in torso-fitting Lacoste shirts and well-tailored madras bermudas, usually sockless with loafers. Winter would eventually coax them into crew necks and baggy chinos.

Despite Jeff's modest, impecunious background, he and these other elite boys were bound together by their cherished membership in something that was long-established in Louisville but had been recently outlawed up in Toledo – a high school fraternity.

Frats and sororities had been banned up there due to an intolerable buildup of juvenile delinquency during the years after World War II, a phenomenon which officials blamed on what had become autonomous, gang-like societies which had completely subverted academic life. The Greek groups were replaced by faculty-advised "service clubs" confined within each individual school, with meetings, dances, and other approved activities fully monitored by adults.

But in Louisville, both male and female societies flourished – funded and controlled by networks of Old Boy and Old Girl alumni, vying for members citywide in schools, public and private, and flaunting Greek-letter or other flamboyant names.

Jeff''s group was the *Semper Parati Literary Association,* the oldest and most prestigious.

Like the others it was provincially snobby and, despite a few high-sounding cultural or community projects, devilishly social. To be sure, the *Semper Parati* guys were the butt of jokes about Boy Scouts and "being prepared" – and thus had been nicknamed the Preppies.

The Preppies published an expensive, felt-covered literary annual full of juvenile essays on God and country, the evils of Communism, or the joys of hunting. It featured photos of all the brothers, formal and candid – in tuxedos or barely concealed behind locker room towels – plus mildly ribald cartoons celebrating individual escapades or peccadilloes. There were pages of congratulatory displays from such kindred organizations as the Athenians, Gamma Zetas, Chevaliers, and Pirettes, or from local advertisers like "Jack Krotzer's Orchestra, Society's Favorite."

Literary or not, each edition was full of any red-blooded Preppy's four favorite conversational words: "damn," "hell," "ass," and "make-out." Jeff gave Teddy a copy of the treasured tome, inscribed in a tiny careless scrawl, "Best wishes always." He still has it.

Teddy became smitten with Jeff and the Preppies, that October week, for obvious reasons – and, likewise, Jeff with Teddy because of that precious driver's license and the unrestricted availability of the white convertible. After school Teddy would drive Jeff downtown to buy some new piece of athletic gear, or even a book; they'd buzz directly down there and return the long way around, the more time Teddy could spend with Jeff.

Though Louisville was larger and more populous than Toledo, Teddy found its physical mien utterly banal by comparison. Toledo's pinnacled cluster of office towers, soaring suspension bridge, smart hotels, and glimmering theaters made it seem almost a snippet of lower Gotham. Louisville's endless, treeless grid of brownish brick boxes – hotter than Hades in summer – turned its back on the town's one scenic asset, the turbulent Ohio.

Ironically, within another couple of decades this lusterless moth would metamorphose into a twinkling skyscrapered Oz, especially at night – while Toledo's aesthetically bankrupted core would sleep through those same decades pocked with boarded-up landmarks, weedy parking lots, and various ill-sited, architecturally timid horrors of "urban renewal."

After their downtown errands Teddy, at Jeff's direction, would drive east... past legions of shabby old shot-gun houses and along the meandering river road through a section of lordly wooded estates... in and out of the Country Club, to see if any girls were grabbing that last bit of sun around the still-open pool... then away from the river into Indian Hills – a nakedly new enclave of sprawling "mansionettes" set amid artfully landscaped hillocks, with sweeping circular driveways, pineapple-topped gateposts, and three-or-four-car garages. Many of Jeff's fraternity and sorority friends lived here – each with a set of indulgent, often absentee, parents. It was a grandiosely exaggerated version of Teddy's own genteel milieu back home, yet the young people living here seemed so much less intellectual, so effusive and blatantly frivolous. For them, every day was their birthday and every night Halloween.

Jeff piloted Teddy from one elaborate homestead to another, introducing him to Gary, Terry, Buzz, or Brad... Ham, Harry, Bruce, or Stan. They joshed endlessly about sports, booze, girls, and fellow fraternities. All of them exuded a certain salty friskiness in a crowd but, exasperatingly, never in intimate circumstances. Transfixed, Teddy faked great interest in their extroverted activities and was tolerated by them, he suspected, only because of Jeff.

On the last Friday afternoon of his visit, Teddy drove Jeff and four other Preppies, jammed onto each other's laps, into the city's vast Frederick Law Olmsted-designed Cherokee Park, then down to the lake where a station wagon full of girls awaited them, like sirens or – Teddy thought upon meeting them – harpies. For the first time ever he felt an intense, visceral disgust at being among female company. He perceived them as rivals, threats even.

Just being in Cherokee Park stirred up two provocative reminiscences, although Teddy had not been there in a quite some time...

The first was memories of long-ago family picnics beside that very lake... sultry Sunday affairs fraught with scratchy seersucker, boring fried chicken, pesky flies, tittering old aunts – and tittering old Cousin Cecil, a wizened, leering little man who was a highly respected undertaker and who took a special fancy to Teddy. (Teddy suspected why, but didn't learn the truth for sure until he was much older.)

His favorite male cousin, Tommy – a former *Semper Parati* who ended up singing opera in New York and would, one day, die of AIDS – snickered to him all about the sanctimonious Cecil, who had amused folks for years by flicking his cigarette ashes into a hideous urn on his desk containing the cremated remains of a deadbeat client... and also had been renowned, in very special circles, for throwing wild midnight parties featuring gay porno films from Havana!

A more poignant recollection was simply that Aunt Silvia once had lived on a street just above the park and, although Teddy was warned never to venture there alone, he did so anyway... there to discover his one secret sanctum in the world.

Sliding down a deeply-shaded slope along the park's very edge and pushing through a labyrinth of dew-drenched lilacs, he had come upon a little round goldfish pond, seemingly bottomless, its cold limestone oculus rimmed with feathery moss. He'd lie down, staining his shirt, and study its oblivious, iridescent denizens as they glided among the lily pads, and ponder whichever of life's enigmas was troubling him that day. Then he'd have to go, clambering up and out of the forbidden place. He'd done it only a few times, but had never forgotten.

Now somewhere near that spot again, with Jeff and the Preppies and the brassy sorority sisters, Teddy wished that he could just blink and reappear – with Jeff alone – next to the little pond. Instead, he listened to the gang cooing on and on about sports, clothes, booze, and parties – including plans for that very evening's all-night "orgy" at someone's house whose parents were golfing in Scotland.

Then and there, Teddy devised a doctrine that would guide him for life.

He looked around and envisioned – surely before any of them – that most of these handsome, hedonistic specimens would gravitate to possibly very good colleges (or, if too dumb, work for Daddy)... come right back home and marry each other, raise snippy little Preppies and sorority sisters just like themselves... and go play golf in Scotland.

He vowed never be sucked into such an undertow of conformity, no matter what class of society he ended up in – marriage, kids, and Sunday school were out!

But sure enough, despite retreating to the rather more sophisticated climate at home, Teddy would soon find himself questioning these very same patterns of submission among his own peers. He did this not because he was antisocial – indeed, he had made himself unreservedly outgoing – but because he had become addicted to an arch kind of snobbery that looks down upon ordinary behavior.

Moreover, his attitudes by then were forever colored by his romantic orientation. By the time he reached his twenties, Teddy had learned to negotiate a tightrope – toppling hard sometimes – and to deal with the wildly unpredictable reactions his homosexuality triggered in others, and especially to negotiate the purely opportunistic but fleeting eroticism that insinuates itself into simple comradeship. His perfected technique came to be maneuvering potential lovers into making the first move.

Today, in Cherokee Park, these inclinations were just emerging. Remembering the aborted initiation by his cousin's farmboy friends the summer before, Teddy wanted nothing in the world that afternoon but to elicit an encore with his prized new crony – if necessary in his mother's car.

After the lakeside group broke up, and the boys who had snuggled in with Teddy and Jeff went home with the girls, the two were alone to drive in the gathering twilight back to Saint Matthews. Both had been invited to "the big orgy." A chilly gust raked the copious canopies above, showering them with autumn's first leaves.

Cruising slowly along the curving roads, Teddy could hardly believe hearing himself tell Jeff, in lurid detail, about the rites performed for him in the big red barn and how he was – *ha ha!* – rescued from debauchery by Belinda. Bravely grazing his companion's muscular thigh, he asked Jeff whether the Preppies sometimes liked to do things like that...

Reddening, brown eyes startled like a deer's in headlights, Jeff moved closer to the passenger door, like a frigid date. But he did squeeze Teddy's arm and reply, "Maybe we'll find out tonight."

After supper Aunt Silvia's phone rang. It was Jeff, advising Teddy, rather offhandedly, that attending the evening's festivities was not going to happen.

The football coach had learned about it somehow and, furious, had sanctioned Jeff and his teammates from going out the night before Saturday's big game. He also pledged them to go to bed early. "So... have a good trip home if I don't see you," he signed off.

Teddy actually felt a great relief, not having to face those nauseating girls... but he also felt sad and defeated. Had he detected hostility in Jeff's tone? Or just the diffidence of a guy passing information on to an unimportant acquaintance? After awhile he took a nocturnal stroll around the block, glancing toward the dimly lit Hatcher living room, TV flickering... then up at the dark window of Jeff's bedroom, wondering if he was really there.

From home, the traveler penned a copious letter, thanking Jeff for their good times and the autographed annual. Months later came a sloppily typed, brief reply – full of "damn," "hell," and "ass" – boasting of New Year's parties, getting smashed, and making-out. Teddy still has the letter, pressed in the tattered book, but has no idea what became of its writer.

His fond wish, someday on a family visit, is to escape from them and search the darkling edge of Cherokee Park for that little goldfish pond and – *Semper Parati* this time – take a photo.

*   *   *

IV. LA FONDA DEL SOL

By the time handsome Teddy Chase had come of age in the early Sixties, he was ready to tackle all those urges which had been efflorescing since the day in that Kentucky barn (and some other, barely-remembered, backwoods Michigan experiences which would haunt him later).

Unfortunately, so far, he not only had failed to survive his first bout with college or to embark on some kind of meaningful career at home, but he also had received the dreaded military draft notice... plus a sexual wake-up call from the perceptive Miss Rachel Morrissey. All that withstanding, he lunged headlong into the classless, free-fall world of voluntary enlistment.

While at first curious about officer status, Teddy quickly figured out that he would be happier free of the constraints of an officer's training and lifestyle. Higher education could resume later, though "later" in the life of such a young person might well lie somewhere beyond forever. As it turned out he would graduate from a very good school, in his own good time.

So far, Teddy's erotic interest in other males had been primed by raw hurried trysts in dormitories or parked cars – yet the emotional attachments – love? – which he believed should enrich these acts had never materialized. He was innocent of any but animal coupling, until just before his departure for boot camp.

Meeting Frank on a dark street outside Toledo's notorious Scenic Bar, a place Teddy had never summoned the courage to enter, was the best going-away gift he had ever got.

Frank was a stocky, movie-star gorgeous, jeans-clad guy in his late twenties – a Catholic school gym teacher, of all things. Highly articulate, with a master's degree earned from a football scholarship to Texas A&M, he chose to live simply with his very conservative old parents across the river in the Hungarian section of town. Teddy and his society friends never went over there, except as "slummers" to a tough blue-collar bar called T-Bone's, the only club in northwestern Ohio where live rock-and-roll music was performed.

Contrary to many a silly Hollywood movie portraying the Fifties or early Sixties, rock-and-roll was not yet played at the country club – and certainly not at the senior prom, where Teddy recalled, in the case of his own, that the sponsors insisted on dreamy Glenn Miller. He also distinctly remembered that – unlike in those movies – only the most nerdy girls really had worn pony tails, Peter Pan collars, or twirly skirts with a poodle sewed on the side. The popular, sexy girls wore slinky pegged skirts they could hardly walk in, partially unbuttoned blouses with the collar turned up, and hair styled, like the boys, in dovetails. Society girls were a world apart. Without exception they wore pleated Glen plaid, real pearls, and pageboys caught up in barrettes... and would continue to do so until they were very old ladies!

Frank climbed into Teddy's car after some friendly curbside small talk, and the two drove around for miles, out into the country, conversing deeply about practically their whole lives. They pulled over on a deserted farm road. Teddy, hugely attracted to Frank but afraid of a rebuff, did not initiate their first contact. The more practiced Frank, sensing Teddy's temerity, gently asked permission then kissed him hard on the mouth and enfolded him ardently, for what seemed like all the rest of the night.

It was, at last, Teddy's first truly passionate connection with another man, and it was all he had dreamed it would be. They didn't do much else, physically, that session; but Frank arranged for them to spend the whole next evening in an obscure motel he knew, where they plunged into the first lovemaking Teddy had ever done without feeling like a pervert. Despite his enlistment obligation, he was ready to spend the rest of his life with Frank!

This experience filled Teddy, day and night, with that giddy anticipatory rush which comes on the way to a date with someone with whom stupendous sex is guaranteed. His liberator regaled him with assurances that queer exploits were very common – further confiding that he and his college-jock buddies had often sampled the charms of Texas football's cutest and most famous star. But Frank's ardor had cooled by their third meeting, and he wisely did his younger pupil one other favor – scrupulously, tenderly, explaining to him that, while sex is fun and infatuations can be maddening, you can't allow yourself to fall in love with every willing partner.

"You can stay great friends," Frank gently admonished, "or just nodding acquaintances. But love is so special, so all-consuming... and it has to be so mutual.. that it's the last thing you should deliberately go looking for."

Teddy absorbed this advice but soon forgot it, much to his misery in the coming months.

His first adventure out in the great world, an early crucible for Frank's theory, began near the end of basic training at an army installation in New Jersey. Still confined to post with the other fledgling privates in his group, Teddy was glumly sipping a Saturday afternoon soda at the Main PX snack bar, listening to "Soldier Boy" and "Palisades Park" on the jukebox, when a godlike, dark-haired, dark-eyed young corporal in crotch-hugging tailored fatigues suddenly crossed the room and asked to join him at his little round table.

"Hi, guy. My name's Harvey... Harvey Malitz from New Yawk," the good-looking soldier said. "You look like you could use some company."

Not only luscious but *lovable,* the stricken Teddy thought. Moments after they began getting acquainted, he realized that his new companion's knee was softly, fearlessly, pressing his. Teddy gamely nudged back and Harvey suggested that they walk out onto the sunny, empty parade ground nearby.

Talking there, out of earshot of anyone, led them to lie down in the new spring grass, almost touching but not noticeably so from afar. Harvey proposed that he and – he laughingly emphasized – a straight buddy planned to drive down to Philadelphia that evening for a movie ... and would Teddy, *pretty please,* come along?

Aware of the controversial lesbian theme of the film, "The Children's Hour," Teddy eagerly agreed to go (although he would've gone with Harvey to see Bugs Bunny) as long as no company cadre were around to see him leave the area.

Harvey and his friend were members of a reserve unit, not Regular Army, and could enter and exit the post as they wished. Tucked in the rear jump seat of the buddy's MG, Teddy had only to duck down when they passed the sentry box, and he was free for the night. So off the trio sped to Philadelphia and engrossed themselves in the drama on the screen, while in the dark Harvey grasped his mesmerized new comrade's hand. After a beer or two, they headed homeward.

Kneeling close to the back of Harvey's bucket seat, Teddy first allowed Harvey to massage the front of his pants for awhile by casually reaching around behind, out of view of the driver. Then he let Harvey feel all the way inside and stealthily jack him off. Teddy couldn't reciprocate, except to massage Harvey's right thigh a little and lick the back of his neck. For both, it was an especially thrilling ride and far too brief.

Meanwhile ever since they had met that afternoon, Harvey told Teddy all about himself. He was Jewish but not very religious... graduated from high school with fairly good grades... currently worked as a runner in Manhattan for a Wall Street brokerage... lived with his parents in Queens. Conspiratorially, he also whispered to Teddy that he and a couple of gay pals had just acquired a "crash pad" in Greenwich Village, a great place to party and take tricks. Then he implored Teddy to spend the very next weekend with him in New York.

The training unit was to be awarded their first and only three-day pass that particular weekend, so Teddy accepted with delirious pleasure, jotting down his host's two addresses and the Queens phone number.

Sunday morning Harvey and his friend were released from reserve duty, but before going home drove over to Teddy's company: "To make sure you didn't get into trouble for going out last night."

In a deserted upstairs squad leader's room, Harvey grabbed Teddy and devoured him with a soulful french kiss that surpassed even those of Frank's in that country motel. That sealed the next weekend's plans, and Teddy could hardly wait until Friday afternoon.

Butterflies cavorting lightly in his stomach, he dressed in khakis, Brooks Brothers shirt and tie, and one of his preppy tweed jackets from the ill-fated Old Lyme Shop back home, then feeling like Holden Caulfield's twin boarded the train in Trenton with his small overnight kit. Heading for the cushy club car, he found himself the youngest person occupying it and felt terrifically sophisticated. He lit up a Kent and ordered a very dry martini, and another, as the train jounced along through Princeton and other whistle stops whose names had landmarked his youthful readings of Marquand, O'Hara, and Fitzgerald.

A fortyish, striking-looking woman across the aisle began chatting with him as if she were his Auntie Mame, and Teddy almost pictured himself going off in her Bentley once they arrived in New York... to her *pied à terre?*... to the St. Regis?... to Long Island? But no – red-faced at even thinking about why he was coming to this city – Teddy bade the beautiful, slightly sad stranger good-bye as they stepped out in the cavernous Pennsylvania Station and were engulfed.

He gave the taxi driver the number of Harvey's pad on Sullivan Street and leaned back. Teddy was no novice to Manhattan, having been there several times with chums from his expensive college in Ohio. Their venue had included ten-room Fifth Avenue apartments, meeting for drinks under the clock at the Biltmore (the legal hard-drinking age in New York in those days was eighteen), and chauffeured forays into Midtown under cover of night to see the latest Edward Albee play, or films like "Last Year at Marienbad," or to catch some jazz.

Teddy loved the glossy, towering ziggurats of this world... their fragrant, elegantly appointed lobbies and dusky nocturnal wallscapes of softly glinting windows high above the hoi-polloi... veiling the secret lives of myriad, unknown, no doubt fascinating, inhabitants. Now hurtling down raucous Seventh Avenue, through the sun-dappled brick-and-stone maze of Chelsea, and veering suddenly into the dank, shadowy Sullivan Street was a new adventure.

Arriving at exactly the time Harvey had specified, Teddy found him there on the front stoop, fresh from work in his striped Oxford shirt, bow tie, skintight Levis, and sneakers. "From his belt up, a runner's gotta look business-like," Harvey mugged... "and from his ass down, he's gotta rock an' roll!"

Leaping up the sagging staircase and negotiating a dingy, zig-zag hallway smelling of pee, Harvey proudly ushered his guest into his refuge from home. It was undergoing a frenzied, disorganized spate of redecoration, knee-deep in as many beer cans as paint cans. Its sole amenity was a street view shielded by a beach-towel curtain. Furnishings were few... red light bulb, scuzzy old refrigerator, battered stereo, and spunk-stained king-size mattress.

Dropping the sackful of paint brushes he had brought, Teddy's host engulfed him with the tenacity of a boa constrictor, and the beguiled one ceased to care about their surroundings. Before things got too sloppy, Harvey abruptly backed off and announced – surprise! – they weren't going to stay there after all. Harvey's parents had, that very morning, taken off from LaGuardia for a week in Miami, so arm-in-arm the two *compadres* descended into what was Teddy's first rocketing subway ride, out to the Malitz family apartment.

Emerging in the twilight on Queens Boulevard and turning down a side street, Teddy was all the more captivated by the vastness and variety of New York. Here was yet another facet to absorb... endless blocks of undulating Georgian and Tudor facades, their pleasant curved bays and diamond-paned casements warming the blue-black-gray. Legions of lollipop trees, ringed with spiky little iron fences, guarded the sidewalks and entrances as staunchly as the occasional uniformed doormen. Why, Queens was almost swanky!

The vestibule was claustrophobic and smelled like knishes, but once up the elevator, inside the shag-carpeted, luxurious if overstuffed flat filled with huge fat lamps, there was plenty of room for two hot new lovers to unwind. First Harvey mixed potent drinks from his father's bar, then flicked on the hi-fi console to blast forth his fondest new acquisition, the movie soundtrack of "West Side Story." Finally, engorged in atmosphere, the two leaped out of their clothes and lunged into a fierce bout of acrobatic sex in Mr. and Mrs. Malitz's elephantine master bed.

All the while Teddy was being voraciously licked, starting with his big toe, he was enthralled with Harvey's dancing eyes and suave body, hairless except for his thick tousled mop and the silky thatch around his cock and under his arms. It was Harvey who, unlike previous rougher partners, gently – delectably – introduced him to the proper nuances of fucking, in all its classic positions.

Famished after a soapy reprise in the shower, the pair wandered out to a gaudy all-night coffee shop on the Boulevard, where Harvey knew every sexy guy in every booth. Arm-in-arm, they sprinted back home for more amour, but it was decidedly less spontaneous.

Saturday morning Harvey made an elaborate breakfast, leaving the dishes in the sink. and they set out for a place called Bergen Beach down in Brooklyn – more strange new vistas for Teddy. Harvey declared that there were probably more gay or bisexual men in Brooklyn or Queens than in all of Manhattan, but that most of them stayed right there close to home and mama.

The two went horseback riding over the coarse brown dunes and through junkyards full of demolished cars and rusty, hulking machinery that looked like a giant's discarded toys. Greenish, faintly ominous waves swiped at the breakwater, yet the whole took on a curiously bleak beauty, an "Ashcan School" painting come to life.

Packs of cute, hoody youths they encountered along the way were all acquaintances of Harvey – current or former tricks, he gleefully bragged. Any or all would be willing to make out with Teddy, Harvey teased – even for free. Part of Teddy did want to in the worst way, but a more addled part recklessly disregarded his old tutor Frank's advice in these matters... and ignored the possibility that fun-loving Harvey, sated with his new conquest, was willing to casually pass him off to others. Instead he devotedly clung to Harvey's arm, and Harvey shrugged.

That evening was the zenith (and the nadir) of the visit. The fellows hopped onto the subway for Manhattan, to meet more of Harvey's friends at the city's currently most sensational new restaurant, La Fonda del Sol.

Sixth Avenue had recently been rechristened "Avenue of the Americas," and La Fonda, a kind of showcase of the project's intent, had just opened in a soaring, dramatically glassy corner of the street's most prestigious new office tower. The restaurant's cuisine was a highly designer version of Mexican, an exotic novelty back then when only French, Northern Italian, Hungarian, and Szechwan were acceptable to urbane diners. Its svelte all-white Formica decor, sensual lighting. bewitching mariachi music, and colorful, artfully presented food conjured up by frisky, lithe young waiters attracted a glamorous following dressed in anything from black tie to Harvey and his gang's version of the Sharks and the Jets. The place seemed light-years away from the Plaza's stuffy Oak Room, remembered by Teddy from another life it seemed, or a Schrafft's.

On top of all that, it was incredibly cheap! Eating and drinking in this flamboyant setting, with this unembarrassed gaggle of young guys around the large oval table they had commandeered, was one of the most enchanting – if brief – times Teddy had ever had.

Except that Harvey, goaded by the others, brayed endlessly about his own charm and prowess... recounting how almost every day, on his runner's rounds, he was having the most terrific sex with comely young businessmen in elevators, executive toilets, or on the boss's sofa... and with other runners, construction workers, and street boys in back hallways or wherever! Looking back, Teddy cannot believe how immature he must have been to be so hurt by Harvey's blunt but completely honest portrayal of himself.

After dinner the pack introduced Teddy to the rancorous, sordid milieu of Eighth Avenue and Forty-second Street... *"Queer Capital of the Whole Fuckin' World!"* the guys all shouted joyously enroute, kicking up their legs like chorines.

It was a bizarre circus where anything was possible, with little vice-squad interference.

Part of Teddy loved it, but again he was crushed to see that Harvey knew everyone there, too. He made dates for the next night and the next, while trying to convince Teddy to pair off with one after another of his lusty, willing companions. Finally very drunk, dizzy, and repulsed by the crudely groping, drug-sniffing denizens of a tenement-flat party they had ended up at, Teddy pleaded with Harvey that they call it a night. They rode home to Queens in sullen silence and slept apart in Harvey's room, in his twin beds.

After a perfunctory cup of stale coffee next morning, Harvey quietly stated that he had plans which kept him from spending the rest of the day with Teddy. Guiding him down to the subway and to the correct line that would get him back to Penn Station, he bade his weekend fling an affable but very pat, "So long, it was fun." Before darting back up the stairs, he indifferently suggested that maybe they could get together sometime later that summer.

Graduating with his comrades the next weekend, Teddy hitchhiked home for a few days of leave and a lukewarm assignation with Frank, then boarded a train for communications school up in Massachusetts. Months later in August, he was invited by some barracks mates to share a ride with them down to New York. Morosely longing for – but vaguely dreading – a reunion with Harvey, he accepted in a flash, then thrust a handful of quarters into the PX pay phone.

"Hello... Mrs. Malitz?"

"Yeah, who's this?"

"It's Ted Chase, a friend of Harvey's. Is he at home?"

"Nah-h... Harvey's at the beach with somma his cronies, so he says."

"Would you please give him a message... that I can come down to New York on Friday and visit him, at his apartment?"

"His what? "

"Harvey's place, in Greenwich Village..." blurted Teddy – discerning as he said it that Pandora's box had flown open. Apparently Harvey's folks were in the dark about their son's alternative accommodations. "Um, well..." Teddy continued queasily, "please tell him I'm coming."

"Oh-h-h, I'll tell him, all right! ... He don't pay me room and board, like we ask – and he's got another *apah-h-ht-ment?* "

Bam! Mrs. Malitz hung up. Well, mused Teddy, how could I know?

Feeling even more skittish than before that other trip to be with Harvey, Teddy waited until Friday noon when he and his fellows embarked on the hectic drive from north of Boston to a sultry, grid-locked Manhattan. The buddies planned to stay at the Thirty-fourth Street YMCA, a sleazy faggot's nest that even boy-crazy Harvey had cautioned Teddy against... but he jocularly told them good-bye without passing on the warning, and hailed a taxi for "his girlfriend's" in the Village. The driver wasn't buying it. He smirked when Teddy gave the address as, come to think of it, had the other cabbie on that happier day when he made his first visit. "Girlfriend, eh?" he chuckled.

Teddy didn't care. It was oppressively humid, and he felt more and more disquieted as the vehicle crawled toward what might be his denouement. A few dogged blocks from the apartment, he could stand it no more; he paid, scrambled out, and ran with his little shaving kit, sweating, until he reached a totally transformed Sullivan Street.

In the gathering dusk, Italian lights twinkled in great arcs over the thoroughfare. Accordionists and trumpeters blared, fireworks burst, and frenzied mobs hollered, shoved and boozed their heads off, oblivious to the god-awful heat. It was some kind of carnival, new to Teddy, who was still a couple of years from discovering the delectations of many a New Orleans Mardi Gras. Looking up at Harvey's building, he saw half-naked young men hanging out of all the windows, laughing and motioning the world inside.

"Harvey here?" asked Teddy of an insouciant, lipsticked young man he recognized from the night at La Fonda.

"Sure is... but he ain't gonna be thrilled to see youse," was the answer. Teddy's heart sank and the butterflies fairly pummeled his stomach walls. Any foolish optimism vanished, overcome as he was by desire for Harvey.

"Waddya tell my mother, you dumb fuck?" was his beloved's greeting at the door of the still bizarrely appointed flat. "My old man kicked me out, thanks to you! Now I gotta live all the time in this crappy dump, buy all my food, do my laundry!!!" Harvey was really angry. "...And you're not staying! I got a cute blond number coming down from Riverdale, any minute now."

"Harv... I'm really, awfully... sorry! I didn't know..."

When Harvey fully comprehended the penitent's flood of tears and uncontrollable shaking, he softened but determinedly led Teddy back down to the street, giving him a brief hug and the hint of a kiss. "It's not gonna work out, guy. It was nice knowin' ya... Have a great life! Here comes my little blond..."

With that, Teddy found himself alone amid the carnival's chaos, with a billfold full of cash and a free weekend in the world's most vibrant city. Red-eyed, all he wanted to do was get out. He trudged all the way uptown to the Port Authority bus terminal, another hellhole that Harvey once told him to avoid at all costs, full of vile predators and just plain nasty old men.

He bought a ticket to Boston and fought off an army of rapacious creeps in the waiting area, one of whom actually tried to forcibly kidnap him. (Teddy always looked years younger than his age.) Dozing fitfully through the pre-dawn bus ride, he found himself enjoying a late Saturday morning breakfast in the elegant deserted dining room of the Ritz-Carlton, resplendent in acres of blue stemware and views of the sunny Public Garden – far from grungy Sullivan Street.

In fact the farther he got from Harvey, the better Teddy was beginning to feel. That very afternoon, at a student hangout in Cambridge, he met someone almost as beguiling... a godlike, fair-haired, Kennedyesque coxswain whom he would, weeks later, artlessly treat just as Harvey had treated him. Frank was so wise – this time!

Still it took Teddy awhile to get over his virgin infatuation. He even wrote a rambling poem, set in a cadence remarkably like contemporary "rap" and rich in Gotham's sights and sounds... the lollipop trees, the wan slap of the surf along junkyard beaches, and graphic suggestions of what he and his idol did together. He showed it to his closest, most intellectual army school buddy, who thrust it back: "Tear that up, it could get you kicked out!"

Despite countless other sojourns to New York, in the service and later in life, Teddy never laid eyes on his beautiful, smooth-talking weekend lover again. It also never occurred to him to darken the door of La Fonda del Sol again, or to wonder about its fate... how many bank branches, travel agencies, and Chinese buffets have occupied its choice corner site.

But he does remember, with a pang, the single hour there around that oval table as vividly and tenderly as the fireflies on Rachel's lawn, the strains of "West Side Story," and the laugh and silky smell of young Corporal Malitz.

*   *   *

V. WEXFORD HALL

During military service and his first years as a civilian journalist, Teddy bumbled through a serendipitous Sixties love life. His bedmates numbered in the hundreds, maybe a thousand. Masters and leatherboys in Germany, sailors and marines in Norfolk and Virginia Beach, doctors and dancers in Manhattan... cowboys and junior execs in Dallas, cabin boys and lifeguards in Miami, auto stylists and hair stylists in Detroit. Headlong exploration of the seemingly "classless" gay world thrust him into liaisons with young men of almost every calling – poet, florist, sax player, hardware clerk, illustrator... army MP, naval attache, skating star... college boy, farmboy, trust fund baby, penniless hitchhiker.

He especially relished Atlanta, a superficially proper but hedonistic city then on its way to becoming the San Francisco of the South. The mind-set there was "candy-ass yuppie," a cornpone version of the New York gym-bunny. Had Teddy met the right mate, he might have remained there forever.

But one radiant New Orleans afternoon in 1968, just after Mardi Gras, Teddy did meet his life's partner and soul-mate... a statuesque, hazel-eyed young architect from Chicago named Rick.

Over time, Teddy and Rick recounted to each other most all of their personal milestones of erotic experience. In Teddy's case, this included that riveting first peek with the frisky twins in the Kentucky barn, the beginner's lessons in finesse from the hunky school coach Frank, and his first red-hot lover, the slick New Yorker Harvey.

One tale – that of the first long-lasting, purely *physical* turn-on with a guy – did not occur to Teddy until he and Rick were thirtyish professionals, living in Chicago, and on their way to a hiking trip through the Blue Ridge Mountains.

It was summertime, sometime after lunch. Their silver Porsche roadster belched and geared down to climb the narrow blacktop ribbon that wound beguilingly up the flank of a commanding wooded promontory in rural Ohio. Atop the hill

45

they stopped in the middle of what seemed to be a sleepy English village, clustered across the road from a park-like assemblage of vaguely ecclesiastical, fairy-tale buildings of soft gray stone. Spires and turrets poked here and there, places where Rapunzel or Rumpelstiltskin might lurk. Except for a barefoot band of children hollering across a distant green, the scene was deserted.

This detour was a nostalgic whim of Teddy's. The travelers got out of the car to stretch, and, Teddy purposefully leading the way, found themselves sitting on the stone steps of Olde Montagu, the odd-looking gothic hulk in which Teddy had roomed during his last term at the vaunted all-male college that his parents had sacrificed to send him to... and which he had dropped out of, resources spent, the spring before coming under the spell of the Old Lyme shop, the Morrisseys, Lauramor, and the army recruiters.

Though after bonding with Rick in Chicago and working his way to graduation from Northwestern, Teddy had remained a loyal contributor to his old school. He'd never been back to the tiny campus, perched on its aloof pinnacle miles from the nearest county seat – and he wanted to show it to Rick, whose alma mater was a huge state university.

After musing awhile on the clammy stoop, which was impervious to the warming July sun, Teddy suggested that they take a stroll and he'd show Rick exactly where he'd encountered a very special culprit in his pantheon of seducers... Arnie Sorrell. Rick sniggered and said he could hardly wait.

Olde Montagu stood facing north, at the head of a mile-long pathway upon which all the college was tangent. Teddy extolled the features and foibles of each landmark as they gamboled along, closer and closer to the specially prurient one at the other end of the walk... Wexford Hall.

They passed various ivy-covered academic and residential buildings, the latter carved up into cozy dens for the half-dozen exclusive Eastern fraternities which gave the school its social panache. They passed the Commons, where the campus denizens wolfed down all their meals at long carved wooden tables – raucously served, course-by-course, by white-coated student waiters (usually on scholarship) and lorded over by a "high table" of nabobs. Rick, the architect, was amused by the gigantic iron-hinged portals at the dining hall's entrance, which Teddy said cracked and groaned nightly against the impending stampede of restless, starving animals in crew necks yelling "Moooo!" until – *bam!* – they flew open and admitted the mob.

Next was the church with its mossy, vaguely teetering tower – Anglican, of course – to which all except the Jewish students and finicky Catholics had to report, in jacket and tie, each dour Sunday morning or else receive academic demerits.

Then came the manorial stone "cottage" where the college president's family lived. Teddy had earned some of his expenses as one of the president's coveted student chauffeurs, employed to drive him in the college Buick to and from the airport and to fetch lecturers, honored guests, or important alumni. Teddy recalled being entrusted with the lives, luggage, and idle chit-chat of such people as David Reisman, Lionel Trilling, and the Duchess of Windsor.

Then came Montagu Tavern, where one could escape the bovine doings at the Commons and have a dignified dinner and martini for about five bucks; and in the cellar next door the Kampus Kupboard, a preppy little shop which kept Teddy and his fellows clad. In those days twenty dollars bought a Scottish sweater or three Brooks Brothers shirts, postpaid. The uniform of the sartorially cool was: button-down Oxford shirt, Harris tweed jacket, chinos or jeans, and engineer boots – but no overcoat, no matter how blustery!

Next stop was the college bookstore, presided over in Teddy's day by the acid-tongued wife of the school's wittiest professor (or so his large, sycophantic following thought him to be). She was slender and waspish, with thin penciled eyebrows and a swept-up pompadour like Bette Davis in "Now, Voyager"; he was pudgy, bald, and bearded with a riveting, Rasputin-like gaze and ever-present smelly pipe. The pair cut a swath through academe and the social jungle which made "Who's Afraid of Virginia Woolf?" seem like a kid's cartoon. They livened up many a party with slurry drunken spats – and each was reputed to be having an affair, unbeknown to the other, with the same male student (whose identity was anybody's guess).

Sex and alcohol could be a deadly duo, there in the boondocks. The brilliant young English instructor who had personally convinced Teddy to attend this school died shockingly with one of his students – a star athlete – one boozy dawn after a house party. They were found nude in bed together, the gossipy ambulance drivers reported, after a faulty gas furnace had asphyxiated them.

Still another stop on Teddy's tour were the bland shoeboxy freshman dorms, which even off-season smelled of old socks and too much jerking off in the showers. Teddy's entering class had been slightly too large to be squeezed into these barracks, so he and about a dozen others were assigned, by lottery, to rooms in forbidding, castle-like Wexford Hall – plunked at the very end of the campus promenade, the farthest hike from anyplace. Many roomers acquired bicycles at once.

At first the Wexford gang felt sad, even ostracized, over their fate, but before long they developed their own special camaraderie. It was the quietest place on campus to hit the books, sleep, or contemplate the infinite, and the rooms were shabbily romantic. Unlike the newer concrete-block cubicles their classmates shared, the Wexfordites reposed in huge, elaborately paneled chambers with lofty window-seated bays and baronial, if drafty and disused, fireplaces.

Rick and Teddy finally plopped down on the venerable front steps of Wexford, surveying the mile they had tromped as though looking back through the large end of a telescope.

Rick queried, *"Well...?"*

Arnie Sorrell was, without his glasses, a good-looking Jewish boy from New Jersey... blue-eyed, dark-headed, lithe. Unlike the stocky, smooth-skinned Harvey whom Teddy would meet a couple of years down the road, Arnie was tall and slightly hairy, especially his torso and thighs. Also unlike Harvey, he was shy and soft-spoken, at least on the surface.

Teddy had not been particularly attracted to him, nurturing instead hopeless crushes on a platoon of other comely lads. But one night during a study lull when the guys were all gathered for a bull session in somebody's room, laughing and bantering back and forth over outlandish feats of female conquest, Teddy caught

Arnie looking at him intently. Both flushed. Those steely eyes, flecked with a hint of mischief, followed Teddy's every move until the group split up and Teddy went back to his room at the opposite end of the hall.

He hopped onto his bunk and, in the light of a single study lamp, wearing only briefs and a tee shirt, knelt there in his favorite reading position – propped up on his elbows – and perused a list of Latin prepositions. The heavy door closed and a floorboard creaked. Hot breath whisked across the back of his neck, and he felt Arnie's strong, wiry arms envelop him.

"What's all this stuff about girls, Teddsy?"

Teddy gasped in shock but moved not an inch. Arnie pressed himself up close against Teddy's backside, caressing his bare skin under the tee shirt, and sensuously shoving his huge hot cock into the crack of his butt, nothing between it but their underwear.

"Wanna have some fun?" Arnie breathed into Teddy's ear.

"Yeah, let's go for a walk," murmured Teddy, hardly believing that, for the first time in his life, he was absolutely going to get what he'd been craving. After pulling on some jeans and loafers they met on the stairs and descended, out into the nippy November night.

Wexford Hall brooded at the very edge of the college grounds, which fell away instantly into dark scary woods beyond which baleful moonlit farmer's fields rolled on, seemingly forever.

With the dormitory lights still in view but obscured by thick tree trunks, Arnie turned and fell to his knees, pulling up Teddy's shirt and wetly tonguing his chest and nipples. Before long he eased down Teddy's pants and began licking his stomach, then his cock and balls. He slurped them hungrily up and down and spit on his middle finger, sliding it up Teddy's ass, massaging it as he went on sucking.

Teddy could only stand there, legs apart, stroking Arnie's luxuriant hair and his ears. Almost ready to ejaculate, Teddy pulled back and Arnie stood up, urging his partner to perform all these delectable acts upon him... which he did, admirably, although he nearly choked on Arnie's ramrod of a dick. Near climax the two stood pressed together, slippery belly to belly, and rubbed deliriously until spent – just as the Hester twins had done years ago in the barn. Laughing, Teddy and Arnie headed back to the dorm, having agreed to make time for more "walks" soon.

A few nights later they did it again, but with a lot less pleasure. Annoyed and jittery, they had to curtail their rutting almost entirely because the sanctuary was invaded by passersby of all kinds... married students clumping to and from their off-campus housing, rowdy fraternity brothers visiting their mystic lodges in the woods, and who knows who else?

Next afternoon Teddy walked around and around Wexford Hall, looking up at its battlements and wondering if it could offer them some hidden refuge. He knew there were attics, but getting to them would be difficult and noisy. Heading for the cavernous basement, he felt more inspired. Room after empty, moldy-smelling room led finally to what he was searching for. Midway up in a wall of the innermost chamber was a funny little cupboard-like door with a simple wooden latch. Opening it, he climbed inside and discovered a long, low passage that led through three or four more storage rooms, also too low-ceilinged to stand up in and lit only by grimy-paned, tiny windows in the foundation. In the farthest room was a pile of ancient but remarkably dust-free mattresses, stained with the wet dreams and hanky-panky of grads gone by. The window here looked out on exactly the spot where Arnie and he had entered the woods the other evening.

Teddy could hardly wait to show his eager buddy the passage that night and, groping and crawling their way for perhaps fifteen minutes without the risk of a flashlight, they found themselves lying on the mattresses, completely at ease. Stripping nude, they spent a good hour desultorily indulging in all the techniques Arnie had shown Teddy standing up in the woods. This time Arnie produced a little bottle of baby oil and initiated Teddy in male-to-male fucking. They took turns at it fervidly – doggy style only, not the more amorous face-to-face. That would be Harvey's specialty, a few years later.

50

The horny twosome visited the hidden room often for the rest of the year, but one thing that Teddy wanted did not happen. Not that he *loved* Arnie as he imagined he could love others whom he was lusting after, but he would have liked to cuddle him, kiss him, and tell him something of how much their intimacy meant.

But Arnie was strict. He sullenly repelled any endearments or kissing, even on the neck – calling stuff like that "girlish." When Arnie and Teddy returned to school the next autumn as sophomores, they met for sex only once.

Unwisely and inexplicably, given his family's financial situation, Teddy had brought a car to campus, an old convertible. He and Arnie no longer had access to Wexford's mattresses because the building had been reassigned to – of all things – the divinity department.

One evening they drove out into the ghostly farmlands and had a fitful, hurried, suck-and-jack-off session in Teddy's front seat. Nervous about discovery, cramped and uncomfortable, they also probably felt somewhat jaded toward one another except for the climax.

Arnie made polite excuses for rejecting Teddy's invitations after that, and Teddy didn't truly care – except that he always wondered whether Arnie had found someone else to do it with. He never asked, for he didn't want to acknowledge the possibility of jealousy, an emotion that even his supremely huggable future tutor, Frank, would not prepare him for.

According to the college alumni directory, which Teddy assiduously keeps up with, Arnie went on in life to become a certified public accountant, residing in the New Jersey suburbs with a wife and four kids.

"So, that's it..." Teddy sighed. "That's all, about this place."

"Let's go," nudged Rick playfully. "I'll drive, and with luck we can sleep in Cincinnati tonight... and we'll do all those things Arnie wouldn't!"

* * *

51

VI. LOCUSTS AND LUST

Not long after the "Wexford Hall" revelations, Teddy decided to regale Rick with what would be his most grotesque sexual saga – conjured up by yet another nostalgic road trip.

During the Fifties, the Chase family would while away the summers at a placid, crescent-shaped lake way up in the Michigan woods. Their rented cottage was breezy, rustic, and spare – completely different from the Stockbroker's Tudor establishment back in Toledo. Teddy's mom and sisters weren't pleased about the primitive kitchen and bathing facilities, but the doctor, an avid bird-watcher and barefoot snoozer in hammocks, loved the place. Besides, he was busy with his practice and commuted to the cottage only on weekends.

Though fresh from his caper with the randy twins in a barn, teenage Teddy was interested in a number of things besides other boys. He was especially loony about derelict old houses, and he was a keen student of all the nuances of Victorian styling and decoration, inside and out. He collected antiques, sketched or photographed houses, and loved exploring them.

Dozens of examples slumbered along the narrow country roads between the little burgs the family drove through... Adrian, Blissfield, Palmyra... weaving their way up to the lake. Everywhere stood weathered farmsteads, boarded up or stuffed with hay, porches crooked or tumbled into ruin, empty windows staring hostilely as if the beholder were the cause of their bad fortune... houses that hinted of bygone birth, death, and happy Christmases with horse-drawn sleighs. In the towns lurked gabled, turreted monstrosities of spalling brick and dully glinting stained glass, iced over with malevolently ornate gingerbread, like giant moldy wedding cakes.

Teddy's favorite such place was near the lake, along the lonely two-lane blacktop to the nearby town of Brooklet. The highway made a sudden bend to the left, just before an ominous grove of huge old chestnut trees. Suddenly amid those trees arose the weathered gray portico of a tumble-down, late Greek Revival house from about 1870, its triangular pediment and tall slender chimneys stabbing the sky. Massive square wooden columns marched across the front, and incongruous, Gothic-looking window eyebrows frowned. The heavy paneled front door, mildewed nearly black, was flanked with the remnants of sidelights glazed in blood-red panes, as was the arched fanlight above.

Set back from the road on slightly elevated land, its surrounding farm buildings collapsed, the house loomed menacingly in its dark coven of chestnuts and seemed to say: "Stay back, or you'll be sorry."

And stay back Teddy always did, until one night at the end of the summer when he turned eighteen, his family's last summer at that lake...

Every season he had harbored a crush on the Kuntz brothers – Lloyd and Lyle – local country boys whom he hung out with up there. Lyle was the older one, awesomely virile and gruffly aloof. Lloyd was Teddy's age, hunky and winsome with a straw-colored mop, green eyes, square jaw, firm bulge in his dungarees... and a mischievous streak that made him seem capable of most anything.

Teddy was Lloyd's only city friend, and Lloyd was amused at how adventuresome their boating and frogging exploits seemed to him. Teddy liked gently catching the rubbery things, but then Lloyd would gleefully whack their brains out and pluck off their legs for his mother to fry. Teddy always winced and looked away.

But there was a reward, if Teddy stayed around... Sometimes Lyle, whose black hair, blue eyes, and wedge-shaped muscular trunk made him even more attractive than Lloyd, allowed the younger pair to watch him jack off on his bed. Looking them straight in the eye, he did it sprawled with shirt open, pants down, faintly hairy legs splayed wide, in tantalizing slow motion. He'd lick his own nipples, fondle and stroke his cock, balls, and hard round butt. Dribbling gobs of spit on his thick, stiff rod as he worked, he'd turn over and let Lloyd – but not Teddy – spank his ass until it was red, then finally yelp and spew creamy cascades all over them.

Both brothers were well experienced with girls, but Lloyd spoke of them contemptuously. He frequently hinted that he wouldn't mind messing around with Teddy, in his "den" under the earthen crawl space of his family's ramshackle house. But the part of Teddy that wanted to leap right under there with him still remained bridled, as it had been with those many tempting boys in Kentucky and at home.

The Kuntzes were poorly educated, their conversation rife with "He don't" and "We ain't." The one time Lloyd sent Teddy a letter, he printed so like a first-grader, in pencil, that it was barely decipherable. Largely because Teddy was such a snob, the chums drifted apart and didn't see one another again until the very end of that last summer.

Just about to enter college, Teddy had fooled around with enough guys that he felt he was ready for Lloyd... but he couldn't get up the nerve until his family's very last afternoon, a sultry Saturday, to seek him out. Driving over in his mother's convertible, he found a more fetching than ever eighteen-year-old Lloyd sprawled on the porch steps, grinning in rapt recognition.

"Hey, fuzz-nuts, long time no see!"

He had always called Teddy that. It was a good sign. They clasped arms and Teddy made excuses for waiting so long to visit, evaluating his reception. Then a plan occurred to him.

"Is the old house on the bend still there?" Teddy asked, knowing very well that it was.

"Sho' is, boy," Lloyd drawled.

"Well... I've never been inside it. Wanna go?"

Lloyd looked at him for an instant, green eyes dancing, and answered, "Sho' enuf, boy... I'll be your tour guide." Then Lloyd took over as planner, "Let's go tonight, just before dark... that's the best time."

Teddy's heart nearly jumped out of his chest. He couldn't believe this spin on his invitation and began springing a boner right there.

Lloyd, gazing down at Teddy's lap, went on: "Tell your folks you're staying with me tonight... but we'll sleep out there, in the haunted house."

"H-h-haunted?"

"0-o-oh, yeah... I'll tell ya all about it when we get there... when we're all alone."

They agreed that Lloyd would pick Teddy up a little after nine, and Lloyd mentioned that he'd scrounge up a blanket to crash on.

Later that afternoon Teddy rode into Brooklet with his mom, just for something to do. The county's entire population seemed to be there... farmers, their wives and kids, teenagers, old folks, summer people from the lake. They mobbed the dime store, feed store, movie house, Dairy Queen, and auto repair place.

While his mother shopped for their final cottage dinner, Teddy wandered into the drug store, feeling more and more queasy about the night to come – but also more bold. Peering down through the glass-topped main counter, he spied stacks of packaged condoms, all types and sizes. Though he'd never rolled one on before, he thought that having some would be a good icebreaker with Lloyd. He'd know all about them... maybe demonstrate!

Pointing to a box of Trojans, he nonchalantly chirped: "I'll take one of those" to the blowzy, gum-smacking girl behind the counter.

"You eighteen?" she snickered at her red-faced patron. But she believed him, without torturous interrogation, so he grabbed his purchase and spurted out of there, conscious of raucous laughter. The skag would never have taken that tone, Teddy fumed, with the crowd of macho young toughs in levis hanging around the magazine rack. He bet that she called them over for a good laugh at his expense.

Later on, watching the Jackie Gleason show, Teddy mentioned to his parents the overnight plans, not that he needed permission. He knew that Lloyd's house didn't have a telephone; they used the pay phone at Elsie's Confectionery, half a mile down their dirt road.

"Be back before noon, son. We need to pack up by then."

Teddy's heart was pounding nonstop as Lloyd pulled up in his brother's battered pickup. Leaving by the side screened door, he purloined a couple of extra pillows from the linen cupboard, to add a touch of the deluxe to the slumber party.

Along the way Lloyd indeed told Teddy more than he cared to know about their destination. "We're heading for the old Jarrott place," he intoned. "Do you know why it's been empty like that?"

"Nope."

"...'Cause 'bout thirty years ago, or so, Ole Lady Jarrott kilt her whole family... with an ax, in the middle of the night. Then she just disappeared... ain't never been seen since. But that there house was fulla bodies – her brother and her brother's son, the son's girlfriend, and their bastard kid. Some people thinks they hear that kid wailing... in the woods, where they found its head."

Despite the hot airless night, Teddy shivered. Lloyd grabbed his leg playfully and chuckled diabolically. They were wearing only tee-shirts and cutoffs, and the hand felt electric on his skin.

Suddenly they were there. Heat lightning illuminated the Jarrott place like a monstrous ship made of whitened driftwood or maybe a saw-toothed, gaping whale. Pulling up in the weed-choked yard and gathering their sleeping gear, the fellows contemplated the ruined Parthenon of a house and, just as they were about to enter through a side porch, a siren chorus of locusts screamed out from the trees all around:

"E-e-e... e-e-e... e-e-e... e-e-e!"

Another heat flash – a rather lengthy one – and both looked up and swore they saw, in an upstairs front window, the gaunt face and form of a woman.

"What'd I tell you?" Lloyd rasped. "That's just a ghost, though... It can't be her. She'd be way too old, now."

Possible sex with Lloyd or not, Teddy almost bolted for the road. They looked again, and naturally she – or it – was gone.

Inside they went, eyes adjusting to the darkness, a greenish light still lingering in the sky outside the few unboarded windows. The interiors were bare, except for tattered shreds of wallpaper hanging down like Spanish moss, scattered heaps of dank clothing left hurriedly behind, and some vagrant's beer cans.

Smells of piss and old plaster were momentarily stifling. In the front hall, the heat lightning made a lurid glimmer in the red fanlight. It was thrilling! Still clutching the stuff they brought, Lloyd leaned very close to Teddy, his cigarette breath positively intoxicating.

"Let's explore upstairs in the morning," he whispered. Teddy glanced up and saw why. The steep forbidding staircase with its bulbous newel post swept up into the blackness – to a huge gap near the top where about a dozen treads were missing, caved into the basement along with much of the heavily carved railing.

"E-e-e... e-e-e... e-e-e!" wailed the locusts, sounding something like a small child.

They felt their way back, to a large square room at the rear which contained a musty double mattress, more clothing remnants, some graffiti... W A N D A S U X... and a massive purplish splotch in the corner and up the wall.

"Let's bunk in here," Lloyd said, "if you don't mind that blood, yonder. You know... the murders, probably."

Tossing their bedding onto the mattress, they lay down in the sweltering gloom. Though paneless, the window afforded no breeze, only the last of the greenish light. After they shed their tee-shirts and moccasins, Teddy went further – peeling down to his white jockeys, which were brand new for the occasion and seemed to glow in the dark.

"I got no underwear," Lloyd giggled.

"So? You'll be even cooler than me," Teddy quipped – persuasively, he hoped. He was! After Lloyd wriggled out of his cutoffs, Teddy fished the box of Trojans from his pocket and pressed it into Lloyd's moist hand. "Here's a toy for you... a boy toy."

"I'll show ya what to do with these... in a little while," Lloyd purred approvingly, cigarette breath in Teddy's ear; then he placed Teddy's hand firmly upon his stomach, just above his swelling cock.

One other appealing thing about Lloyd was his skin texture. Smooth and sallow from head to toe – not lily-white below the waist like most guys – he had a slightly sweaty, slippery feel, like he'd just been massaged all over with a tiny bit of baby oil. But he smelled good. Teddy's fingers played lightly down into Lloyd's curly pubic bush, over his velvety thighs, and around his balls and slick, slightly crooked hard-on.

Lloyd sighed and rolled onto Teddy, planting him with an incredibly sweet-tasting french kiss that seemed to last for an hour. Teddy nuzzled his way down and began sucking on Lloyd's cock slowly, as Lloyd rubbed Teddy's hair, working his head up and down. Then Lloyd sat up and roughly stripped off his partner's briefs, wrestling him into the sixty-nine position – something Teddy had only dreamed of. He began licking Teddy, like a big dog, and also worked a spit-covered, muscular thumb up his rear, gently massaging him with it. Teddy used his middle finger on Lloyd, and they had a sensuous four-way rhythm going, until… creak!

The sound came from the room above. The boys were on the opposite side of the house from where they had glimpsed the apparition in the window; but there it was again… creak.

They froze in their embrace, not letting go of each other's cocks yet.

Another creak sounded from the very edge of the ceiling; then another, partway down the wall. They noticed for the first time a framed opening in the room, with a slightly-ajar door opening inward. They were sure also of a faint flicker of lantern shine, coming closer.

"Backstairs!" hissed Teddy's frightened tour guide, spitting out his limp wiener. They jumped into shorts and shoes and scrambled out to the truck, leaving behind Mrs. Chase's pillows, Teddy's virgin jockeys, and the unopened condoms.

Both adventurers remained virtually mute the whole way home. Lloyd dropped Teddy off and, as with most of Teddy's other memorable boyhood satyrs, they never met again…

So, many years later while driving across Michigan, the longtime lovers Rick and Teddy indulged the latter's sudden inexplicable hankering to revisit that serene, silvery lake.

It was remarkably familiar, yet a little bit spoiled. The homespun cottage, along with its neighbors, now had a paved driveway, garage, basketball hoop, glassed-in porch, and bright ugly aluminum awnings, signs that all had been converted to year-around residences. The ancient sycamores leading down to the dock were gone, leaving that once-shady vista naked and nondescript. Elsie's store was now a Jiffymart.

All of those scary old houses Teddy remembered on the way through the boondocks had vanished too, except for the few now gussied up into pricey bed-and-breakfasts. They headed out along the road to Brooklet, and Teddy's heart began its old thump. He told Rick why and Rick laughed, wanting to hear more.

Nearing the distinctive curve with its brooding chestnut grove, Teddy felt yet another pang of disappointment. The Jarrott place was *gone,* except for two blackened phallic chimneys. The property was inaccessibly overgrown out to the highway, and traces of faded yellow "crime scene" tape barred the way through the toppled gateposts.

They pulled aside and Teddy reiterated the whole story of the Kuntz brothers, ending salaciously with the episode on the mattress. Rick, intrigued by the eeriness of the spot, suggested that they try to find out what had happened there... and soon they found ourselves in town, poised before the information desk at the county library and historical society.

There a birdlike woman wearing a bun and pointy glasses met their inquiry with a hard stare, but in short order presented them with a dog-eared manila folder containing three items.

"Used to be a lot more in here... but it's been culled to the essentials," she croaked knowingly, then retreated.

The first thing in the folder was a cracked, oval nineteenth-century photo of the familiar square-columned portico, with a horse and buggy in front and a pyramid of family members posed on the steps. Off to the right, as though deliberately spoiling the symmetrical tableau. stood a gawky young girl with high-button shoes and partially hooded eyes which nevertheless bored right through the picture's beholder. She was identified, in spidery handwriting, as Emilie Jarrott.

The second item, a yellowed news clipping from 1927, was headlined: *JARROTT FAMILY AXED TO DEATH.* It graphically described the killings and the puzzling disappearance of the sole suspect, Emilie.

The third clipping, by an effusive local reporter and dated exactly one week after Teddy's short-lived romantic tryst, read: TWO *BODIES FOUND IN BURNED JARROTT HOUSE. Murder has reared its hideous head again at the haunted Jarrott homestead. Two naked bodies, bound together, bludgeoned, and partially scorched, were discovered today after a late-evening fire which destroyed the 80-year-old landmark, abandoned since Emilie Jarrott butchered her family there* a *generation ago.*

Yesterday's victims were Lloyd Lee Kuntz, 18, of Brooklet Township, and an unidentified male of approximately the same age, thought to be a hitchhiker seen with young Kuntz from afar that afternoon. Authorities grimly refuse to disclose further details. Funeral arrangements are incomplete.

Because Teddy truly hadn't thought deeply about Lloyd since that locust-riven night, he was all the more sickened and stunned by what he and his companion had just read. Reading it once more, he shivered, just as he had when Lloyd first touched him in the truck outside that house. Somehow he knew better than to probe further.

The erstwhile detectives – Nancy Drew? The Hardy Boys? – left the file on the counter and sped away, out of Brooklet, in the opposite direction from the Jarrott place toward Chicago and home. Down the road a few miles, Teddy began feeling much better.

Squeezing Rick's hand, he managed to reflect, "Lloyd musta been really horny to go back there... I hope he got to use those rubbers."

*   *   *

61

AFTERNOON IN THE BALCONY

I.

The beginning of Brad's lifelong nightmare came about in Miami Beach during the spring of 1965, just before his twenty-third birthday and just after his discharge from three years as a military news correspondent at Fort Benning, Georgia.

Still harboring warm feelings about his army friends, Brad could have chosen to ease into the fact – the shock, really – of his utter new freedom by settling in the nearby town of Columbus, a sleepy old place by no means devoid of charm and intrigue. After all, Fort Benning had been the setting of *Reflections in a Golden Eye,* and Brad himself had spent shadowy late afternoons at those very stables from which Carson McCullers's anguished lovers saddled up – himself riding in fatigues, almost daily, deep into the antediluvian woods with an untalkative, hard-muscled barracks buddy from West Virginia who, using copious spit, would bend Brad over a fallen oak and ram the daylights out of him.

Brad's closest straight friend, J.B., had just married a vivacious, liberal-minded Columbus girl who treated Brad like a brother. J.B. had also become managing editor of the city's daily newspaper and had offered Brad the job of police reporter. But, oh no! Brad knew – or thought – that this venue surely would prove too stifling for the adventuresome, well educated *bon vivant* that he was. His local gay acquaintances were hopelessly rooted by tenacious family or business ties, doomed to lives of transient dalliance with Fort Benning soldiers; and he'd had enough of pool-side trysts at the Holiday Inn or the Martinique – and more than enough of unpredictable, but usually gratifying, cat-and-mouse entrapments of straight-appearing guys at the seductively lit Ralston Hotel bar.

Reflecting back weeks afterward, Brad regretted not taking up J.B.'s offer.

He might also have sought his fortune in his favorite – in fact, addictive – weekend retreat, Atlanta. Picturesquely hilly and bucolic and not yet scarred with twelve-lane freeways, it was an alluring hotbed (behind the screen of musty manors and glinting skyscrapers) of danger, glamour, and serendipitous amorous possibilities – as well as a country boy's New York for career opportunities, judging by the fact that nearly everyone you met there was from somewhere else.

Peachtree Street, in the Sixties, was a visual and sensual parade day or night – from way downtown by the campy old Rialto theater, past such spiffy emporia as Rich's, Muse's, and Davison's, then the Hyatt's brutally beautiful new atrium-lobbied towers; past the famous Fox (hulking, tawny brick, onion-bulbed Ali Baba fantasy then hosting rock concerts) and the original Krystal (hamburgers 5¢) and the Cabana Hotel, its driveway lined with life-sized erotic Greek statues; past the site of Margaret Mitchell's imposing girlhood home and the now-queer art cinema in front of which a speeding taxi snuffed her out – and still onward, past pubs and boutiques, taunted by the fat tumescent tower of Saint Philip's Cathedral in tony Buckhead. It was a young, good-looking guy's Via Venito, Sunset Boulevard, and Forty-second Street rolled into one.

On Sundays when the bars were closed, and if you had not been invited to one of myriad private champagne brunches gay city dwellers loved to give, you had to be inventive. Arriving in Piedmont Park around eleven in the morning, you'd cruise around the jewel-like lake in your car, or on foot and presto! – along the sinuously curving "Spanish Steps" or down on the sequestered sunbathing pier you'd find an afternoon's, or even a lifetime's, companion. Often you'd find your ride back to Fort Benning, if you needed one, and some romance along the way.

Yes, it was the obvious place for Brad to settle since he was bitterly determined not to go home to Ohio and his parents, whom he had not yet forgiven for their midstream cutoff of college finances, which had forced him to enlist or be drafted. And yes, he lacked the courage to offer himself up to (be swallowed alive by) one other place familiar to him, Manhattan.

But more than a couple of his Atlanta relationships had soured at just this crucial time. He felt so unwelcome there that, based on the really convincing invitation of Paulie, a cute, surfer-blond traveling salesman and recent bedfellow, Brad pointed his thumb toward Miami instead. In the blink of a day and night he was standing on a palmy street corner, phoning Paulie.

Infrastructurally, in those days, Miami was a cerulean-domed, ivory-walled, seaside crescent evoking the Alexandria of Lawrence Durrell. Any hint of culture was discreetly hidden within the enclaves of immensely wealthy householders. People-wise, it was the town of Candy Mosler, brassy wife of a fat old millionaire-maker of bank vaults, who'd been accused of hiring two of her husband's young hustler boyfriends to dispatch him and make it look like an accident. It didn't, and Candy's titillating trial and adroit acquittal by F. Lee Bailey were the sole talk *du jour.*

Sandy-blond himself (also blue-eyed, lithe, and nicely endowed), Brad always looked at least five or six years younger than he was, and as time went by he would look even ten or twenty years his junior. Though precariously short on cash (and he'd rather die than tell his family where he was) he did not lack for a social life – at first, while he was the new boy *du jour.* Not counting the supple, limpid-eyed Cuban boys, he seemed to meet only two types of guys in Miami: those perennially surf-bronzed centurions who drove Caddy convertibles, looked eternally young, and had steady employment; or guys like himself who hitchhiked, were indeed young but not so tan, and had no employment.

Not that Brad wasn't looking for work. He bugged the Florida State Employment Service almost every day, then he'd go hang out along Miami Beach's raffish Twenty-first Street strand; or maybe he'd be a few blocks inland, negotiating that night's love and lodging at Frenchie's Bar, where motherly drag queens served up a free homemade buffet every couple of evenings. On his own he wrangled an encouraging, but inconclusive, interview at the Miami Herald and even left his writing samples with the slightly sweet personnel director (who raised an eyebrow when Brad confessed that he still didn't have a real address at which to be contacted).

The seductive Paulie who had lured Brad to Miami was a Cadillac owner, too, but was lately between jobs and addresses himself. Yet he did finagle temporary occupancy of the spare room of two old Jewish sisters he had known through his sales work. Their little pink stucco hacienda with the flamingo screen door amused Brad, who was allowed to sleep there also when not otherwise engaged. Sexual gratuities to his host, while gladly offered, had to be very minimal because the bed squeaked at every stir and the room had no air conditioner.

Through this connection, Brad landed a bellboy position at Waldmann's, a venerable, strictly Kosher family hotel on lower middle Collins Avenue. It was a stuffy, dour place not at all like its ritzy neighbors, the Saxony, Sea Isle, or San Souci. Truly dreading to even show up there, Brad first interviewed the manager of the classy new Carillon Hotel nearby, but was gruffly thrown out of the man's office for not appearing in a necktie. (At this time, he didn't even own a tie and had only one pair of shoes.)

Thanking God that the Waldmann sons did not make him wear a uniform or a monkey hat – just a clean shirt and black pants – he worked the three-to-eleven evening shift, was paid minimum wage plus tips (ha!), and was forbidden to snitch even one cream puff from the bounteous kitchen just behind the baize door near the bellhop desk. Between wrestling with mountains of luggage and clothing bags toted in with each flabby-faced family from Massachusetts or New Jersey, he had to wait upon the crabby occupants of the Mah Jong room ("Young man, gimme a seltzer!"), assiduously empty the ash trays of even one ash, and, after dusk, watch out that no more than two of the huge jug-like lamps in the cavernous terrazzo lobby were lit at a time. If a guest turned on a third one, then wandered away, Brad had to scuttle over at once and turn it off.

Old Mrs. Waldmann, the bedridden but dictatorial owner, lived on the top floor of a high-rise across busy Collins, and it was Brad's job to lug her jumbo Kosher dinner over each evening at six sharp, rain or shine, in a heavy pail sanctified by the kitchen rabbi. Brad was positive that her sassy black maids spit into the bucket before serving it up.

For all this he received virtually no gratuities. The only staff who really got tipped were the cute-assed, slightly sinister Cuban car jockeys, who gave him the score: "Dem kikes better tip us *bueno...* or d'ole fender gets a scra-t-t-tch."

Three decades later, it gave Brad great pleasure to drive by the haughty Carillon and see that it was defunct and boarded up – and to discover that Waldmann's had been bulldozed flat! Its beautiful beach and pool, forbidden to "the help," was now public. The neighborhood farther down, near Frenchie's, had become the frenzied zoo called "South Beach." Its chromy, marzipan-facaded cafes, jam-full of wannabes in Calvin Klein duds, clutching cellular phones, had displaced the disheveled old retirees in housecoats or undershirts, peering from the cracked jalousies and dismal piazzas that the younger Brad remembered.

One evening at Frenchie's, off-duty from Waldmann's, Brad was feeling the absolute lowest he had felt since coming to Miami. He and his friend had just been given notice by the old sisters not to come back (too much squeaking), and his first paycheck was so small that it wouldn't cover even the cheapest flophouse for more than a night. As for Paulie, he simply disappeared.

Then a brusque, well-built, curly-haired guy – fetching but probably straight – sidled up and bought Brad a beer. They began talking, and Brad learned that his companion was the chief mate on a large yacht moored just around the corner from the bar. He bragged on and on, about gleeful adventures in glamorous Caribbean ports and the expensive accouterments of the vessel.

"Wanna come see it?" Curly asked, pressing insistently against Brad's thigh. "We can have a beer there."

Pressing gently back, Brad cheered up and replied, "Sure, I'm game."

The two walked out along the Intercoastal dock past a jumble of beautiful yet intimidatingly pretentious boats, the waves slapping, ropes and chains clanking. They gazed up at gaggles of cocktail-swilling, sun-fried men and women of indeterminate ages. Climbing onto a vast white sailing craft adorned with polished and gilded wood, beveled glass, and cushy deck furniture, they headed straight below without a hint of a grand tour. No one else was aboard.

69

Down in the mate's cabin Brad's beefy host, stripping away his shirt and jeans, announced:

"I'm gonna take a shower."

"What about me?" intoned a mildly puzzled Brad, looking forward to a soapy session with his new acquaintance.

"No way! I'm not queer like you... but I do want ya to blow me before my shower." With that he kicked off his undershorts and unleashed a thick hard dick, then grabbed Brad's shoulders toughly, pushing him down to face it.

Flushing angrily, Brad pulled back. He was strictly a reciprocal lover (though in his time he had gone along with a few one-sided guys – like his saddle buddy – if they asked him nicely).

"Hey, we do it together or not at all."

"Then not, faggot! ...wait here till I'm done."

Brad waited sulkily, humiliated but too polite to storm out. He thought some more about his situation, suddenly actually missing Georgia – its sylph-like pines, red earth, and rainy nights. So different from the never wavering, hot blue blur of Miami.

The mate dried off, changed, and firmly guided Brad back up on deck, where they sat and he said: "You know, I feel sorry for you... There's an all-gay yacht just down the pier from here. The owners are filthy rich old fruits, who employ only hunky-looking crew members who swing, and they're lookin' for a new boy – I know. They're sailing for Ocho Rios tomorrow and... if you want... I can get you hired."

Brad had told Curly enough about himself – crummy job, no degree, no roof – that no wonder he suggested this bizarre way out. Probably many a fellow would grab it, becoming a sore-assed, virtual whore among the lowlife on some fickle old fag's boat – probably to end up maliciously dumped without a dime in some faraway, definitely unfashionable port.

No thanks, answered Brad, he'd take his chances at Frenchie's.

"I'll walk you back," said Curly, his tone considerably softened. Strolling along in silence, they parted at the door. "I won't come in, but here's a buck for that beer."

And he left. Brad's spirits had rocketed and tumbled full circle in that short hour or so. He was feeling dejected again, immersed in his dilemma.

Then his blue eyes locked with those of Dave.

II.

Blue-eyed, trim, nicely endowed Dave – Brad's twin? – had recently migrated to Miami from Iowa, determined to abandon the climate, his stodgy hometown, the memory of his domineering but recently deceased father, and the irascibility of his invalid mother. Just a year or so younger than Brad, Dave seemed to have a much better handle on life. Or maybe he was luckier. He'd already found a well-paying position in the art department at Burdine's, one of the city's flagship department stores, as a fashion illustrator. He also had a snug little furnished apartment overlooking Biscayne Bay, just north of downtown, and a still-snazzy '58 Impala convertible bought for him a couple of years back by his late father.

Though physically similar – and ferociously attracted – to Brad, Dave was otherwise completely the opposite. For one thing, he was cold-bloodedly guiltless and pragmatic. For another, he was incurably restless. He couldn't simply take a good job and stick to it. From the first day he had to wonder what it would be be to work for a *better* store, like Jordan Marsh, or one of the New York stores that were beginning to open branches in the Miami area.

Brad and Dave became lovers the night they met – lasciviously glued together whenever near a bed! In the wake of such a heady infatuation, Brad's troubles seemed to vanish. He now had a place to rest his head, with someone he liked, who seemed to want to care for him and help him. He was able to abruptly, but courteously, sever himself from the bellhop job the very next day because, miraculously, that morning the State Employment Service secured for him a Monday-through-Friday, nine-to-five, slot as the assistant cashier in a prestigious stock brokerage, F.I. du Pont and Company. This meant buying at least two neckties right away!

The position paid not much less than Dave earned at Burdine's, but it was very intense work that made you shut out the whole world, even at lunch. You dealt not with people, but with very vital snippets and pieces and piles of paper that were crucial to them. The yelling, screaming, and heart attacks over those pieces of paper were borne by better-paid higher-ups.

Although it was nothing like the fluid, expansive reporter's work that he had done so well in the army and really wanted to continue with, Brad was proud that his survivor's instinct allowed him to quickly master the variety of complicated procedures and transactions he was responsible for. He particularly enjoyed physically touching, as well as examining and transcribing the crinkly, ornately engraved stock certificates that clients sent in to be traded. Most of all he loved meticulously typing each selling customer's cashier's check for hundreds, thousands, even millions, of dollars. It was like creating funny money. That was the only feature of Brad's job that interested Dave, over dinner.

They went out every night to inexpensive Cuban cafes and umpteen clubs, explored the newly gay ghetto of Coconut Grove, and spent a sand-in-your-underwear weekend down in grungy, still undiscovered Key West. It was an indolent life but not boring. They were faithful and passionate, at first.

As days went by, Dave proved to be not only restless but also unpredicably moody, arrogant, and critical of Brad's passiveness. A mediocre high school performer except for his artistic abilities, he was disdainful of Brad's better education and more upper-class background; and, though he had read some of his lover's writing samples, he did not appreciate them for the simple reason that Brad had not yet persuaded the Herald to hire him.

Dave also had a violent temper and consummate contempt for authority. One evening he mouthed off to a cop, after he and Brad had deliberately broken the city's very strict jaywalking law, and the two were nearly jailed and had to pay a stiff fine. He also would blow up at Brad for no reason, often in public. Once he shoved Brad out of the car in Fort Lauderdale, where they had been bar-hopping, and when Brad finally arrived home via thumb (declining to have sex with his attractive driver), he found Dave in bed with another guy – an ugly one, to boot.

Crushed, and stripped of patience, Brad decided to move out, get his own little place, go on with his brokerage job until the Herald came through, and try to enjoy life. He had even been corresponding with his parents, who actually encouraged him. Not to be bested by Brad, Dave announced that he planned to move to Dallas – his new quest being to illustrate for Neiman Marcus (since only Burdine's in Miami seemed to be interested in him).

The Saturday for the pair to split up came, and Brad had all but signed up for a studio on a pleasant cul-de-sac near the bay. He had dropped off his dry cleaning, as usual; he had deposited Friday's paycheck in his new savings and checking accounts; he was dreading Dave's departure, but being strong. For the last couple of nights the two had been sleeping together, but not touching or talking. At the crack of dawn Dave suddenly took Brad in his arms and, kissing him soulfully as when they first met, implored, "Don't stay here... Come on with me to Big D. I can't go there without you, dummy..."

This made Brad so happy that he did it, unblinkingly. By ten in the morning, car stuffed with belongings, they were tooling across the Everglades, Brad's dry cleaning and his samples at the Herald and his bank accounts all left to be redeemed somehow later. Dave, of course, had taken care of all his obligations earlier that week.

With a disappointed-in-himself pang in his stomach, Brad phoned his kind and very astounded boss at home to inform him of the defection, and he realized that he and Dave were exactly the reason that Florida employers are so skeptical of newcomers.

By afternoon, whizzing along the Gulf coast with the top down, head in Dave's lap, playfully biting Dave's boner through his pants, Brad had forgotten Miami.

III.

Flying westward in the marina blue Impala, pausing only for hamburgers and gas, the fellows pulled into Biloxi in the wee hours and talked the frowzy proprietress of a run-down beach front motel into giving them a "slightly used" room for three dollars. They slept, made love, lazed around the beach, and had a scrumptious seafood brunch, with plenty of beer, at a place Brad knew all about.

Here it was Brad's turn to shine a little. He loved ramshackle old waterfront Biloxi, sprinkled here and there, Coney-like, across the narrow Gulf highway from the stand-offish leeward hotels and oak-shrouded mansions. He had tarried there several times going to or from New Orleans during Mardi Gras, while stationed at Fort Benning. A onetime lover he'd met at Mardi Gras had shown him a whimsically nautical, port-holed restaurant, motel, and nightclub that catered strictly to gays, and was the site of the bounteous brunch.

A few summers later, Hurricane Camille would wipe away all of old beach side Biloxi. Today nothing much is there but vapid sand, pocked with parking lots and concrete-block or steel-piered casinos – skeletal by day, entrancing by night in their shimmering neon skins.

Dave was almost impressed. But he was impatient to shove on for New Orleans, another place he had never been. They cruised into the city along the old U.S. 90 causeway, past miles of colorfully scruffy fishing shacks with improbable names ("Mae's Titties," "Crab Bisk") and over creepy bayous, forested by druid-like dead cypresses. They inched through the wide, hot, cacophonous avenues until they reached the balconied, beguiling streets of the Vieux Carre in late afternoon. Glad to leave the car and wander on foot – again led by the more knowledgeable Brad – they dined at fusty Galatoire's (in jackets provided by the restaurant) and explored the shadowy cathedral, pigeon-pocked Jackson Square, aromatic French Market, and the shuttered yet malevolently enticing antique shops of Royal Street. They had a beer at Wanda's, a renowned hustler hangout where a nearly naked old queen puffed on cigarettes through his buns on top of the bar, and finally ended up at Lafitte's, one of the most famous gay taverns in the world.

By then it was midnight, and Dave was determined to mooch a night's repast. Sure enough he did – from the skinniest, nelliest, most unattractive person in the place. Brad didn't participate in this deal; it disgusted him and he just went along. Their stay, though on a bare mattress, even included morning showers, coffee, and beignets. The price? Sometime during the night, Dave left Brad's side for the bed of their horny host. Brad had been invited, of course, but wouldn't go.

And so... off to Dallas! The pace of the journey was entirely erratic, controlled by the whims of Dave, who didn't seem to have a timetable in mind. They dawdled along down St. Charles Avenue, now racing the streetcar, now zig-zagging through the shady Garden District or Audubon Park; then away from the city at last, westerly along the sparsely traveled Old River Road, its mighty namesake invisible behind the hulking, grass-sheathed, serpentine levees. With Brad driving, Dave glanced toward an eerie jungle-like grove that suddenly loomed on the land side of the road and, peering though a slightly ajar, cyclone-fenced gateway, yelped: "Stop!"

They got out and walked gingerly along the brush-choked allèe, coming closer and closer to the mossy brick arches and rotten columns that Dave's artist's eye had glimpsed from the road. It turned out to be a huge old plantation house – forlorn and threatening in its empty silence, its decay. They ventured inside, where the unnaturally chilly air smelled of urine and crumbling plaster. The main floors were above, but the stairs that grandly marched up there were gone, only a trace of magnificent wainscoting adhering to the wall. Dave ran back for his sketchbook and spent an hour skillfully recording the enchanted ruin, using Brad's rump as a pillow.

Brad daydreamed a bit about the hoop-skirted daughters who had probably flounced up and down those phantom stairs, fanning saucily but sweltering anyway in these isolated, bug-bedeviled environs. He also thought about the vine-strangled, crumbling two-story *garconnière* nearby and wondered what horseplay the damsels' randy brothers or beaus tried on each other, lying up there at night shirtless – and maybe pantless – under their mosquito nets.

Our two vagabonds couldn't know it then, but thirty years later this almost doomed house, "Destrahan," would be nobly relinquished by the chemical company that owned it and become one of the best-restored landmarks on the whole River Road. Brad, who had an amateur student's knowledge of colonial and antebellum architecture, began happily pointing out the building's regional nuances, but Dave just scoffed. His exquisite drawings were all he needed.

Later that afternoon they passed a dingy but still operating old movie theater, its ornate peeling pilasters upholding an entablature embossed – R I E N Z I – the name of the sad little town they were passing through. Brad wondered if anyone living there had heard of the fourteenth-century troubadour or of Wagner's opera. He knew Dave hadn't. On the marquee: B E T T E D A V I S, "Hush, Hush, Sweet Charlotte," 3:00 5:00 7:30.

"I haven't seen that one yet," Brad mused. "I've heard it's really scary."

"Okay, let's go back," Dave agreed, pointing to his watch, which read 2:55. "I'd like to go again – and you'll love it."

Pausing at the ticket window where a slatternly, gum-chewing woman drawled, "Tew bucks, plaize," Dave demurred, pointing to an overhead placard: Main Floor $1, Balcony 50¢.

"How about the balcony?" he asked.

"It's jus' fer the niggers, but yew can set there if yew want," she sneered, looking at them as though they were from another planet.

"We'd jus' love to," gushed Dave, stuffing a sweaty dollar bill into her cage.

After buying some hot buttery popcorn they sprinted up the unswept, unlit stairs – stairs that totally bypassed the lobby, candy counter, and restrooms. They had the entire cool, dark balcony to themselves, except for a solitary black youth in the corner who looked at them once in glum disbelief.

79

The film delivered thrills as promised... Bette's hysterics, Joseph Cotten and Olivia deHavilland's sardonic connivances, severed hands, hacked-off heads, and wisteria-cloaked settings that strikingly resembled those experienced that morning at Destrahan. It also was one of the last really tender times for Brad and Dave. For the first part of the action they intermittently munched and held hands, and for the rest – unzipping, fingers slick from the popcorn – they teasingly, stealthily, stroked each other off.

"We'll do more later," promised Dave, licking Brad's ear as they rose to leave. But it didn't turn out that way.

IV.

"You know, this is the same stretch of highway where Jayne Mansfield was decapitated in a wreck a little while ago," snickered Dave to Brad, who had taken the wheel again. Remembering the nighttime news photos of the roofless black Continental, scrunched like an old beer can beneath the rear of a semi-trailer, he shivered and drove on.

Just after dusk in the middle of nowhere, a stocky, wedge-shaped young figure appeared by the roadside, thumb out. He was nice-looking, wearing jeans and a tee-shirt and carrying a windbreaker, hard hat, and small bag.

"Stop!" Dave ordered. "Where you headed?" he asked the hitchhiker.

"To Beaumont, back to the oil rig I work on," his hazel eyes flashing in gratitude for the lift. "I've been seeing my girl and stayed a little bit late."

Dave motioned for him to drop his stuff into the back seat and told Brad to put up the top. Then he slid over to the middle of the front seat, allowing the newcomer to squeeze in on the right. It was a little cramped so Dave shifted, raising an arm and resting it along the shoulder of the new guy, not Brad. The boy, short-haired and clean-shaven, was very quiet and the three rode, almost without conversation, into the night.

At some point Dave whispered something to their passenger, and the two hopped over into the back seat. The rigger pulled his shirt up, and Dave began slowly running his tongue all over his smooth torso. Glancing miserably through the mirror and over his shoulder, Brad heard more than saw the jeans slide down and Dave's ravenous but measured and expert sucking on the boy's rosy hard cock. The recipient kept his eyes closed, his hands gently caressing Dave's backbone, up and down. Sticky tears stained Brad's face and neck as he drove on, and eventually a tumultanous moment of moaning and scuffling, signifying a mutual climax, came and went, leaving the back seat deadly still.

The pair slept until just a hint of light, then the oil crewman dressed quietly and climbed back into the front seat. He learned from Brad that they were nearing the northeastern edge of Beaumont. Indicating the side road where he wanted to get out, he haltingly grasped Brad's arm in farewell and said, "Hey, I'm sorry." Brad shrugged and waved him off.

Dave didn't wake up until about half an hour after the young man from Beaumont had gone. Exhausted, Brad had pulled off the road into what looked like a gravel drive leading up and back to a dark, old-fashioned Texas bungalow with a rusting tin roof and a porch wrapped around three sides. Rubbing his eyes in the gathering light, Dave mumbled, "Gee, dummy, you need some sleep, too." He always called Brad that. "This place looks abandoned... let's pull up by the house and nobody'll bother us." Another one of Dave's nervy decisions...

So they did, Brad stoically saying nothing about the night's antics. Stretched out on both seats they both dozed deeply, until later that morning.

About nine o'clock, Assistant Deputy Sheriff Sid Vaux drove past the gravel lane to the old Roan place, as he usually did on his way into work in the town of Sour Lake, and noticed a speck of bright blue way back near the house. Nobody had lived there in the decade since Randolph and Ada Roan, a seemingly fit but morose couple in their sixties, had suddenly gotten up from the breakfast table one morning and walked together into the bayou, up to their necks, and drowned. Nobody knew why, and nobody but the suspense clerk of the Probate Court even cared anymore. No kinfolk were ever found.

Curious, but not nearly nosy enough to be a really good cop, Vaux backed up and turned into the rutted, overgrown drive. He got just far enough to see that the strange car seemed to be a marina blue '58 Impala convertible, a car he had always drooled over. He also thought it had a license tag in colors other than those of Texas. He even glimpsed the last two numbers – 69 – which made him giggle, thinking of the women at nearby Mamie's pullet farm and whore house.

"Sid!" a crackling voice snarled over his police radio. "Git in here quick, or you'll be late for your own ceremony!"

"Roger, almost there!" responded Vaux, rudely reminded that today his boss, and the mayor himself, were finally going to reward his years of scheming and brown-nosing with the coveted promotion to Chief Deputy Sheriff – *Numero Duo* over five better qualified men whose surnames, unfortunately, did not happen to link them with the founders of this very Vaux County.

"Maybe somebody's lookin' to buy this place," he mused, heading back down the drive in a cloud of dust. "I'll check it out later."

Even the deputy's intrusion did not awaken Brad and Dave, but they did rise shortly after, rested and hungry. But Dave, always capricious, was intrigued by the somber old cottage and wanted to explore it before they headed onward in search of breakfast.

"C'mon, we've got all day to get to Dallas," he chided.

The windows, gray with dirt and broken here and there, still had raggedy lace curtains or torn green shades, flapping wanly in the light morning breeze. They entered through a warped, slightly open door and found themselves in a kitchen fully furnished with rusting appliances, cupboards stocked with dusty cans and jars. A frying pan full of ancient grease stood on the stove and, most unsettlingly, the table was fully set for two, the plates still streaked with half-eaten remnants. The chairs were pushed back crazily as though their occupants had left abruptly. An overturned juice glass and another, shattered on the floor, completed the tableau.

Wandering into other rooms, they discovered furniture and artifacts in place, family photos, coverlets and counterpanes, all intact but blanketed with mildew and spider webs. Clothes, very out-of-date, ravaged by moths, hung neatly in the closets.

"This could only happen in the South," observed Dave, turning to Brad and, for the first time, comprehending his red-eyed, tear-ravaged countenance. "Ohhh... Hey, Braddie, I'm sorry about last night. The guy was cute... and he let me do it."

Brad's anguished expression made Dave impulsively hold and kiss him as he had not since their first days together.

"Well, ain't they sweet?" barked a twangy East Texas voice from the bedroom doorway.

Two rangy, tousle-haired young men, sexy but mean-looking – dressed in hunting boots and caps – stood there with shotguns pointed straight at the embracing couple. One was a little older than the other, clearly the leader.

"Cousin Bo," he beckoned to his companion, " I reckon we got two faggies passin' through here. Let's get Miss Kissy Face to suck on yer humongeous pecker." The speaker's name was Duane, and he was referring to Brad.

Amazingly, the guns being held on them did not phase Brad one bit. A tremor of ecstacy, not fear, went through him as he obediently knelt before the handsome Bo, who had shyly unfastened his shiny black pants. This was different than with the guy on the boat, Brad reasoned – and he would relish getting even with Dave, watching him out of the corner of his eye.

Bo's yellow-stained briefs and pubic hair smelled sweaty, but the rest of him smelled good. Running his mouth languidly over Bo's engorged cockhead, Brad took his time, also fondling his firm little balls and, feeling between the legs, fingering his surprisingly compliant ass in sync with the sucking. Red-rodded, red-faced – and in no hurry to do so – Bo came furiously, as Duane watched in derision and Dave stared in what could only be called numb incredulity.

"Okey-dokey," said Duane, motioning Bo to help him, "now it's my turn fer some real fun."

Without relaxing control of the shotgun, they bound Brad's hands to the doorknob with an old clothesline and pushed Dave face down on the musty iron bed, pulling off his corduroys and tying his ankles, spread-eagle, to the foot rail and his wrists to the head rail. Duane – who was even better looking than Bo – then stripped completely and, pulling a lubricated condom out of his wallet, unwrapped it and rolled it down over his own huge shaft. Then he shoved it gently, expertly, up Dave and began methodically fucking him, the old bed groaning in cadence and both the captive and his guard watching in fascination.

Brad noticed that the upper half of Duane's narrow-waisted body was a faded, rosy tan from the past summer but that from the belt line down he featured a Roman statue's white alabaster butt and legs – a sign of times when blue-collar males did not yet work or play in any type of shorts, like sissy college boys. The normally petulant Dave chose not to yell, figuring that he would never be heard, but also enjoying the screwing and the sensation that Duane was also kissing his neck, leaving hickies.

Duane's hard round ass began pumping faster and faster, and a minute later he surely burst the condom with his violent climax. He never did mention why he used a rubber instead of going bareback. Brad had never encountered a guy using one on another guy. That would happen a lot in another decade or two. In this morning's instance, it would add spice to a baffling mystery.

Finished, Duane jumped up, dressed, and snarled to Bo: "Have I got plans fer these homos, and Uncle Sid will cream over their car!" They whispered together a moment, then gagged Brad and Dave with dishtowels and led them into the yard. Duane ordered Bo to empty all stuff out of the trunk and toss it into the back seat. Then they forced their prisoners into the trunk, legs bent and feet tied, slamming the lid shut – but it didn't latch because of a shirt hanging over the edge.

Now Brad and Dave felt afraid for the first time. Breathing was suddenly getting a little harder, and their entire bodies began aching at once from their cramped confinement.

"Hey, let's look through their shit, see if they have any cash before droppin' em into Gator Hole," said Duane, apparently not caring whether his prey learned in advance of their dissolution.

"Man, nobody'll know they were ever here," added Bo, speaking for virtually the first time all morning and sounding just as diabolical as Duane.

Now terror-struck, listening to the rustling and unzipping in the back seat, Dave salivated enough in his gag to completely loosen it. He whispered to Brad to try to do the same. Next he asked Brad, whose face was pressed close to Dave's wrists, to untie the rotted clothesline with his teeth. This accomplished, Dave could reach behind the spare tire where a small bag, undiscovered by Bo, was stashed – a bag containing his seemingly bottomless supply of traveler's cheques and a .45 army pistol. He pressed its cold, flattish barrel to Brad's cheek and rasped, "Didn't know we had this, did ya?" They altered their constricted positions considerably, and waited.

"Okay, which'a yew pussies got the car keys?" growled Duane, yanking up the trunk lid and leaning suddenly over them. Brad had instinctively pocketed the keys when he stopped driving early that morning.

Pow! Suddenly, Diane had no face.

Ka-pow! Neither did the startled Bo.

Dave had shot them at such close range that he couldn't have missed. Two slugs through their two pea brains, was all he thought. Fear now gave way to sheer exhilaration. Brad shared these identical feelings, but wondered that God thought. Was there a God?

Quickly the liberated ones unbound their ankles and foraged through the house, returning with quilts – exquisite, old-time country ones – soaked in water from the rainbarrel to sop the speckles of blood off the trunk lid, lining, taillights, and bumper. Brad panted, almost joyfully, "I don't think we actually touched a thing in there, except the kitchen door." (He'd overlooked the bedroom knob.)

"You're so right," agreed Dave, hugging him and sprinting back to swab the door down. "And my old man's gun has outlived its usefulness today! If we're lucky enough to make Dallas, I'm gonna drop it in the Trinity River." (Before studying their road map, he had never heard of it.)

Stowing the firearm back in the bag, they draped the bloody spreads over the remains of the Adonis-like but ill-fated cousins, hopped into the car, and slowly descended the scrunchy lane. Seeing no traffic at all, they turned onto the highway and sped off. It was not yet noon.

Still tremendously elated, they brushed back any notions of guilt, or of the consequences of flight. Who wouldn't? Duane and Bo themselves had set the tone for this benighted place, Dave rationalized. Now it was just a game. Could they make it to Big D and the river, or not? Though awfully famished, they drove straight west, all the way to the new interstate, before stopping at a funny old Art Deco diner in a hamlet called Cut and Shoot.

"Good place for us," laughed the fugitives, as they wolfed down two blue plate specials and tore off up the ramp toward Dallas. As they arrived, that day had finally almost died – the sky a morbid purple, the lights of the dated, ugly skyline glimmering balefully beyond the hideous elevated roadway leading to it over miles of concrete pylons.

Not exactly the Emerald City, but it was theirs! Stopping on a bridge at the very edge of town, Dave hurled the thoroughly wiped .45 and its single clip into the darkling Trinity.

Next morning about nine, Chief Deputy Sheriff Sidney McClanahan Vaux IV bounced into the drive of the old Roan place on his way to work. Until now he had utterly forgotten that he was going to check around there for mischief.

V.

Brad and Dave spent their first evening in Big D driving around, orienting themselves to various landmarks – Neiman Marcus, where Dave was determined to work; the Morning News, where Brad aspired to work; the recently – and now forever – notorious Dealey Plaza near the city's famously queer bus station; the stuffy Adolphus Hotel, its red plush carpeting spewing out into the street, daring the ordinary passerby to step on it. They ate at the Dallas epitome of a classy restaurant – a glossy, chandeliered steakhouse featuring fifty varieties of barbecue.

Later they searched for and found a gay bar that Dave had been told about, Villa Fontana. It was exactly that – a sprawling old Mediterranean house in an iffy neighborhood, built around an open courtyard with tables and chairs, a tiki-hut bar, and a fountain bathed in ever-changing colored lights. Unlike the dumps most gay clientele found themselves imbibing in around the country, Villa Fontana was then very typical of Dallas. The imaginative surroundings evolved partly from the city's lack of strict zoning and partly from the aggressively "yuppie" aspirations of much of the area's active homosexual culture. Drinking was quite incidental – the city's bars then served only beer, or wine coolers; hard liquor was permitted only in "private clubs."

Another tony place, Ex Calibur, was cocooned inside a single-story former insurance complex on a nocturnally deserted commercial back street. It had a dozen rooms, decked out in luxurious castoff corporate furnishings. The little office cubicles had become television lounges, snack bars, chess rooms, reading rooms and grotto-like trysting places. It even had a laundry room... a guy could live there! Then there were the usual hellholes, narrow vomity-smelling old hustler bars in the crummy lower end of downtown near the bus station and Dealey Plaza.

That first beer in the Villa Fontana, thanks to Dave's schmoozing, landed the fellows a free night's lodging with two friendly, talkative lesbians – no strings attached – one of whom provided Dave a job lead at the city's less fancy department store, Sanger Harris. Sure enough, next morning Dave's smooth demeanor and stunning portfolio got him a full-time position in the store's art department. He had been warned away from Neiman Marcus, where it was virtually impossible for an unknown arriviste to even acquire an application form.

Brad could not approach the Morning News without his samples left in Miami, but by that very afternoon the escapees from the Gator Hole of Sour Lake indeed had an address for the samples (and Brad's dry cleaning) to be forwarded to. A dozen blocks out Main Street was a leafy, quiet area of down-at-the-heels clapboard homes and duplexes which was disappearing beneath cheaply-built new mid-rise apartment blocks with soaring glassy foyers, gold-flecked turquoise tiles, courtyard swimming pools, and exotic names. Into one such monstrosity, "Scheherazade," moved Brad and Dave – approval secured due to Dave's new job, security deposit coming from Dave's waning wad of cheques. Moreover, the willowy long-nailed manager, Darlene, seemed to like them. The place was unfurnished except for draperies and a king-sized mattress left by a dead-beat former tenant. Darlene let them have it, with a wink: "Yew boys won't mind doublin' up, I bet?" She also conjured up a halfway decent sofa, lamp, end table, and TV on a stand. Dave taped his drawings of Destrahan to the walls, with the thought of framing them.

Life in Dallas started out too good to be true. Brad and Dave actually behaved like lovers again, as they had in Miami. Brad often posed for Dave's elegant and sexy fashion illustrations, and he loved seeing his likeness, clad in swim trunks or the latest preppie togs, displayed across full-page spreads. Some of their new friends recognized and admired him – to Dave's chagrin.

Brad's employment materialized, not from the Morning News but from a jarringly different source. On a purely survivalist whim, he took an advertised civil service examination for police clerk with the City of Dallas and passed, with not only the highest but also the only perfect score. He reported for assignment at the hulking, blackened old police headquarters building, presided over by the very Chief Jesse Curry in whose face had exploded the JFK tragedy, and he both entered and left the building through the same below-street vestibule where Lee Harvey Oswald had been shot little more than a year before. The finger-printing didn't bother him. He was almost positive he had touched nothing back in the old Roan house.

Despite praise for the high test score (along with cracks about smarty-pants Yankees), Brad's assignment was not a plum. His duties were at the Police Auto Pound office and yard on the scruffy upper edge of downtown – logging in the license plates, registrations, serial numbers, and inventory of loose property associated with each car or truck the Dallas police impounded, whether from abandonment, parking violations, accidents, murder or mayhem. He was also charged with all the bureaucratic machinations of releasing these vehicles to their usually irate owners or their snippy attorneys.

The pound office was a grim concrete shoebox with a clammy floor reeking of Lysol, like all places where the lowest class of public business is done –- jails, morgues, post office lobbies. First thing one morning a tangled clump of black fiberglass, mangled wheels, and a Corvette nameplate arrived for Brad to write up. It was all that was left of a pair of rich college kids who, the newscasters bleated, had been caught going over a hundred miles an hour on the freeway late last night. The sudden sight of blood spatters made Brad momentarily queasy. The families never came to view the car but an insurance guy did, laughing incongruously when he saw it.

It could be a boring or a hectic job, with only fifteen minutes allowed for lunch. Weekends were free, but a daunting clerical backlog had to be dealt with each Monday. Because Brad was low man in the office pecking order, he was often rotated to the evening shift when somebody was sick or wanted off –- usually with no warning. This was highly irriating to Dave, who made all their social plans and whose eye was starting to wander among the comely array of male models, salesmen, and fashion executives that he was beginning to meet.

Brad's workmates were simply the antithesis of Dave's. They included two balding, grumpy old clerks about to retire, who brought their lunches in used paper sacks from home; sharp-eyed, red-haired Sergeant Moore, the uniformed boss of the place who disliked Brad instantly, and a pair of tough young wrecker drivers. One was Smitty -- a skinny, beady-eyed, smart-mouthed shrimp resembling Alfred E. Newman -- who also disliked Brad. The other was Bobby -- darkly blond with flowing ducktails; steely gray eyes with long lashes; slightly downy, chiseled, features like a newly weaned movie star; sinewy neck and arms swelling from his skin-tight tee shirt, and a firm, round bulge chafing assertively inside the front of his form-fitting jeans.

It was hard for Brad to avoid watching Bobby's every move (although he never had enough nerve to follow him into the men's room), and his ruddy presence made the job almost worthwhile. Nobody at the pound seemed to feel other than indifference or contempt for Brad except Bobby, who -- while rather shy and physically stand-offish -- at least expressed curiosity about Brad's schooling and background. Here, Brad had to be the cautious one.

Late one sultry afternoon, Bobby offered to drive Brad home to the apartment in his pickup truck and, dying to see Bobby without clothes, Brad courageously invited him for a swim and a beer. He knew that Bobby lived in Oak Cliff, a white-trash area across the river in which a certain .45 rested and rusted -- a section of town with no swimming pools and few air conditioners. Once they pulled up at Scheherazade, Bobby abruptly demurred from what Smitty would surely call their "date," softly drawling: "Maybe another time."

Brad's relationship with Dave was worsening daily, with Dave becoming more and more arrogant, insulting, abusive -- and absent. Brad began thinking of a way out.

"Why don'cha invite *me* swimming, honey?" Smitty smirked at him the next day.

VI.

When Sid Vaux drove his cruiser up to the old Roan house, he nearly ran over the heap of old rose and green quilts laying near where the blue Impala had been -- until he saw a leg, then an ear. Peeling aside the gore-soaked coverings, he nearly passed out. Mother of God! These lifeless unfortunates were his two no-good -- but lovable and highly placed -- nephews, Duane Vaux and Bo Jenks! Horribly disfigured, their heads were stuck to the earth in a viscous, blackening puddle of coagulated blood. He leaned heavily against a fender and spotted the pair's rifles, scattered nearby.

This moment was the beginning of a very bad year for Sid. It essentially erased the triumph of twenty-four hours earlier as he had passed close to this spot, fully expecting to easily garner worthiness and respect in the eyes of the local establishment -- to which he was born, but which had never taken him seriously. Surely now, he'd never be Sheriff!

Feeling about an inch tall, he realized that this thing might surely not have happened, had he not jumped like a chicken at that snappish radio summons to glory. Duane and Bo surely couldn't have been lying here then -- he had passed them, waved at them, on his way in to the ceremony. They looked to be going hunting, playing hookey from Bo's daddy's sawmill. Sid's crushing feeling of incompetence made him -- for now -- neglect to mention the marina blue convertible as, sobbing uncontrollably, he called his discovery in to headquarters and the coroner's office.

Never in its history had Vaux County seen such pandemonium -- yet only within its swampy borders. Outside, virtually no notice was taken of the double homicide, as that was certainly what it must be. Big-city newspapers across the state gave it two paragraphs. The Associated Press, nationwide, gave it one. But in Vaux County no stone was left unturned, except the one the culpable Sid was sitting on.

The Vaux and Jenks families had such friendly enemies and such inimical friends and relations that nobody in the county, male or female, was above suspicion. The old Roan cottage, left so mournfully undisturbed and dignified all these years, even by Brad and Dave, was ransacked from attic to cellar, peppered to the last doorknob with fingerprints from every busybody for miles around.

The most sensational, inexplicable thing anybody found was Duane's used condom, gummy and glistening, squashed on the dusty floor near the rumpled bed. Equally shocking was the coroner's finding that both young bucks had recently ejaculated lavishly, their crotches smeared with dried cum. Most folks decided the killers had to be women.

Sid didn't have a clue, but vowed to keep his sighting of the blue Impala to himself. Quietly, after hours, he entered its partial description into the statewide "Wanted Vehicles" list, a roster which eventually made its way to facilities like the Dallas Police Auto Pound.

VII.

Brad took steps to free himself from the increasingly savage and indifferent Dave. Amazingly they discussed the events of Sour Lake only once, chuckling a little over the sexual part, and agreeing that the denouement of the cousins was simple self-defense.

One night after last call at Ex Calibur, during a skinny-dipping "pot" party behind the high walls of a rich queen's house, Brad was befriended by a pair of lovers, Skipper and Dale. All three had something in common -- too shy to completely strip, they were lounging together around the pool in their Jockeys. Somewhat nerdy, Dale was likable but not attractive; Skipper, a lifeguard-like, smoothly complexioned redhead with tigerish amber eyes, was irresistible. They invited Brad home, ostensibly to sleep between them, but once there in bed Brad boldly ignored Dale, who, sobbing a little, left Skipper and their guest to go at it. One thought spoiled it a little for Brad – was he turning into Dave?

Next morning after Brad made peace with Dale -- whose affiliation with Skipper was apparently rock-solid -- he looked around their pleasant, well-appointed home with a kind of melancholy envy. He had known numerous couples like this in Atlanta and deeply aspired to their domestic bliss someday, something that could now never happen with Dave.

Still attracted to Brad, the errant Skipper -- his muscular body literally poured into a tan summer suit (he was an insurance appraiser) -- made one more date with him, fetching Brad from work and speeding to the Scheherazade for an intense bout of lovemaking. Skipper liked his nipples and stomach licked, then to be fucked on his back, his powerful hands leaving scarlet welts on Brad's shoulder blades. Afterward Skipper sighed, guiltily: "We can't do this again."

Aware of Brad's blighted home life, Skipper and Dale introduced him to a chum, Buddy, who lived on a secluded street in an interesting boxy, Bauhaus-inspired, four-flat near the entrance to posh Turtle Creek, the city's best neighborhood. One upper studio, featuring a wall of sliding glass doors to a balmy deck overlooking the building's screened-over Japanese garden, happened to be available, unfurnished, for only $75 a month. Buddy put in a good word for Brad with the resident landlady, who was partial to gay tenants, and the enchanting space was his. A pal of Buddy's chipped in a spare platform bed and two yellow butterfly chairs. Towels, pillows, and kitchen stuff were lent by Brad's newest admirer, Larry -- a freckled, fresh-faced college-bound youth whose rambling suburban family home had overstocked linen closets. He eagerly helped Brad cart his belongings from the old apartment, after a tearful good-bye from Darlene. His note to Dave, with a final rent check: "Take care, I've moved."

Clinging socially to the wings of Buddy, Skipper, and Dale -- plus the tireless, succulent cock of cuddly Larry -- Brad was almost happy. But he still loathed his job, and felt less and less hopeful of being hired by the Morning News. Hard-boiled Dallas was so different from the friendlier Atlanta that, despite his refuge among these few new companions, he was finding nothing there potent enough to soothe away the splattered visages of Duane and Bo.

Meanwhile, somehow, the feud between Brad and his parents had mellowed considerably. They missed each other more and more as time passed. Latest letter from Mom: "Why can't you come back, finish your journalism degree here, down the street at our own public university where you wouldn't go before? Live at home, apply for the G.I. bill, and work at our own very fine newspaper? Dad's friend Al Rosenberg, the city editor, has promised you'll have the next open reporter's slot." (So! mused Brad, it truly *is* who you know, not your yellowed writing samples.)

Why indeed? The arrival of an invitation, forwarded by his mother, to take part in the late summer wedding of the first boy Brad had ever had a crush on (unconsummated) fused into action his diverse yearnings for the familiar, for opportunity -- and for escape, if not absolution.

The very next morning he presented a disdainfully smirking Sergeant Moore with a two-week notice of resignation, and gave a similar communication to his landlady -- who was none too pleased, because she had given him such a reasonable rent on a promise that he would stay for six months. Feeling suddenly light-headed, Brad realized that, in just a few days, he might be able to distance himself from the Gator Hole and all fateful post-Miami associations.

VIII.

Located between the auto pound and the downtown police headquarters, where Brad was often sent on errands, was one other notable gay bar, the Zoo. Sometimes between errands he spent his lunch break there, having a beer and a sandwich and parking the city truck nearby.

The Zoo was something like a sophisticated Fifties cocktail lounge, with softly, luridly glowing cornices curving around the room, leopard-patterned carpeting, and zebra-patterned low back stools around the mirrored island bar. Day and night the clientele -- except for a few determined old floozies -- was men cruising men. They crowded in, drinking sullenly, expectantly: clad in business suits, Ivy League tweeds, cowboy hats, levis and boots, biker jackets. Brad had his share of adventures initiated there, but not while on duty. He just stopped to look.

One afternoon he took home a wiry little rodeo star who resembled Audie Murphy. The back seat of his enormous Bonneville was heaped with cans of hair spray -- "Fer mah lariats," he explained. He liked the bottom, and lots of baby oil. Another, severely crewcut guy, resplendent in leather pants and big black motorcycle, insisted on top. He was so hung that it took ten minutes of easing in for Brad to comfortably accommodate him. He rode Brad home more than once.

"Hey, honey," Smitty whispered to Brad one day in the rest room, "didn't we see you comin' outta that there Zoo-bar?" Bobby didn't join Smitty's taunting but just snickered, having had little to say to Brad since the aborted swim date. Brad held Larry all the tighter that night, under black silk Neiman Marcus sheets, on his borrowed bed overlooking the aromatic Japanese garden. Larry was sad that Brad was leaving.

Early the next afternoon Bobby's wrecker clanged into the yard, hauling behind it Dave's marina blue Impala. Brad felt a sharp pang in his stomach, then rallied. A few minutes later Bobby stomped in, sweating, and threw a jumble of stuff from the car's interior onto the counter for Brad to sort, transcribe, and secure. A green cardboard form, partially filled out in Bobby's childlike scrawl, noted that the car had been towed in on a parking violation and that there was nothing in the trunk, to Brad's relief. But he did have to inventory a folio of newspaper ads, figure drawings of a ravishing young guy in his underwear, an umbrella, and a straw boater that the dapper Dave had taken to wearing. On top was a small pile, obviously from the glove compartment: a beer can opener, some colored pens, a much-folded road map, a 1etter, and an old dry-cleaning ticket.

Unruffled, Brad took a small manila envelope and marked it "glove compartment," dropping in only the opener and pens. The map, letter, and ticket he squirreled out of sight under the counter to be dealt with later. The map was a sectional one, highlighted over the exact route he and Dave had taken from Miami to Dallas; the ticket was for the Miami clothing sent to Dallas weeks ago, and the letter was from Brad's mother, containing references to Dave. No longer mad at her, he felt somewhat sorry about having to destroy something she had written to him.

The next thing was hardest to do. Brad first studied the manifest of the day's impoundments to see Bobby's description of the car. "serial number blah-blah, 1958 Chevrolet Impala 2-door convertible, metallic blue, blue interior, Iowa tag number UG 1069." Then with wildly beating heart he checked Sergeant Moore's favorite document, the wanted vehicle roster, for the first time ever.

Nearly all the way down, ready to be dropped from the ever-changing list next time it was mimeographed, came the entry; "58 blu Chevy Impala conv, licensing state unk, incomplete number ending in 69." Next came code numbers indicating the area of Texas where the car was wanted, the date, and type of crime involved. Translation: "Vaux Co, April 30, homicide." The sergeant checked that sheet nearly every day, hoping to become a desk-bound hero!

Not having even seen Dave since moving out, Brad phoned him at the store; "Hello, it's me... Never mind. Why has your car been dragged here to the pound? ...Parked in a tow-away zone while on a job interview with Neiman's? ... Dave, *don't* come for it. Leave it here, *forever*! ...Forget your sketches, and meet me at the Zoo after work. I'll fill you in."

On his way out at shift's end, Brad overheard Sergeant Moore braying into his phone, "Vaux County Sheriff's Office? This here's..." He tore the letter and other items to smithereens and dropped them into a dumpster he passed on the way to the Zoo. Half surprised that Dave was already waiting for him, huddled in a dark booth, Brad explained the implications of the towed Impala. He believed that if questioned, neither he nor steely Dave would pass muster.

"That car's always been in my dad's name and he's dead, and my miserable old lady's in a state home for nuts," Dave recounted logically, nonchalantly. "Nobody can link me to those sketches either, come to think of it. They're of a cute little hustler from Lubbock I took home from the bus station -- didn't have to pay him, either. You're right... let 'em have the old clunker."

"Incidentally," he went on, changing the subject entirely, "I've spent a wild night with your pals Skipper and Dale. I was a lot nicer to Dale than *you* were... he knows the art director at Marshall Field's in Chicago." That knocked home Brad's retarded acceptance that, most of the time, sex was just a door-opener to Dave. Unlike the romantic Brad, he'd do it with anyone who could be of the slightest use. "They told me you're leaving Dallas."

"I would go tonight, if I hadn't given formal notice to my boss before this happened," said Brad. "Come to think of it, it'll look more normal if I just calmly stick it out... *You'd* better take off too, Dave. Don't even tell me where."

"If I don't get that job at Neiman's, I just might take off for Chicago, by my thumb and my dick, just like you."

"Good luck, Dave." Not touching him, Brad stepped out into the sticky Texas night.

IX.

Next day a puffing, perspiring Assistant Deputy Sheriff Sid Vaux (he had been demoted) presented himself to the Dallas Police Pound. He looked over the grime-caked convertible in the lot, ruefully concluding that, aside from the "69," it only coincidentally resembled the shiny specimen he glimpsed that innocent morning weeks ago. Then he asked to examine the interior contents.

Curious about the visitor, Bobby was on hand as Brad emptied the brown envelope onto the counter in front of Vaux and Sergeant Moore. They guffawed at the prissy boater.

"Where's them papers from the glove box?" huffed Bobby, staring at the opener and pens.

"I don't recall any papers," was a reddening Brad's well-rehearsed response.

"Don't tell me there wasn't a buncha maps and crap in there, I brought 'em in!" the driver insisted, angrily snatching the green inventory card to see what it said. The penciled entry only mentioned "drawings & stuff." The damningly unique folio eluded their interest altogether.

"It's a good thing you're on your way outta here," the sergeant grumbled to Brad. Neither of them had yet told the other workers, and Bobby shot Brad a stunned look -- the kind of look that meant, perhaps, that he didn't want him to go.

Vaux didn't know what to think of the car anymore. Nothing about it suggested *female* ownership. Sergeant Moore, also disappointed, sent him home in ignominy, promising to delve into registration and such -- an onerous task in those days before nationwide computer banks. Oh, and to detain for questioning whoever might come to claim it.

"Want a ride home?" Bobby asked Brad, on his very last afternoon at the pound.

"I don't have a pool anymore," Brad replied, "but I might have a beer."

"Good enuf," said Bobby, draping his muscular right arm tentatively across the top of the seat back, inches from his passenger's shoulder. Along the way, driving one-handed, Bobby asked Brad where he was going and why. Not wanting to lie, yet not allowing himself to be specific, he answered in such Odyssean generalities that Bobby didn't press further. But his arm eased down onto Brad's shoulder very lightly.

Brad's hard-on was virtually fighting its way out of his pants, and Bobby's glance skated over it more than once. Up in the shady grotto-like apartment, Brad realized that his final few days and nights there were indeed ticking off. Larry would be coming over later as usual; but right now, sprawled across his slick dusky sheets, nursing a beer, was somebody that he had genuinely ached for.

"I'm real sorry I yelled about that glove box junk," Bobby said quietly. "Smitty thinks one time he saw that Chevy drop you off at work."

Survival instincts taking over, Brad curtly lied, "I told you, I've never seen that car before." He reached around and softly tuned his bedside transistor radio to a country station he thought Bobby would like.

"You walk by, and 1 fall to pieces..." sang a plaintive Patsy Cline.

"That's how I feel about you," murmured Bobby, lunging firmly against Brad's tense body and kissing him wetly on the neck.

What followed was the most sensual sex Brad had ever had – before or since. Bobby dropped his stiff macho pose and melded seamlessly into Brad's every choreographic maneuver, top and bottom, earnestly, without inane utterances. As he tongued Bobby's tight hard ass, Brad felt Bobby's ardent mouth gently, relentlessly, massaging his cock until they both came for the third, then a fourth time. It was nearly dark when he got up to go.

"What Patsy Cline said, I meant it," asserted Bobby.

Here was another temptation for Brad to arbitrarily drop a logical plan and abandon himself to the charms of someone (a probably someday incompatible someone) with whom, for the delirious now, he could just forget the blue Impala -- and just bury his face in that silken belly, ruffle up that fragrant straw-colored mop, cleave to those godlike shoulders, and bounce up and down on that hot red pole.

But no! He wanted no more Daves, who made him jump through hoops for a speck of affection; no more abruptly quitting responsible jobs with people he truly liked, as in Miami; no more Larrys, preparing to go East to school and a whole other life. Besides, the not wholly unsuspecting Bobby lived and worked a little too close to something called Gator Hole, way off in Sour Lake.

"Thanks, Bob... I'll always remember you."

X.

The next evening, Brad's last in Dallas, he came home late after farewell drinks at Villa Fontana with Skipper, Dale, and Larry, who had morosely collected his mother's borrowed bedding and cutlery. Tucked in the screen door was a note from Bobby.

"I came to say good-bye again, but this will have to do," it began. "That podunk sheriff's flunkie said it wasn't no use trying match up that Chevy with whatever happened down there, so forget it. Goody! If that car ain't picked up in another 45 days, I'll get a buddy from outside the P.D. to buy it for me. It reminds me of you."

Brad's Cincinnati-bound bus rumbled northeasterly out of Dallas, over another ugly freeway on stilts, over a no-man's prairie used for God knew what. He didn't glance back. Even the morning sun couldn't gild that baleful skyline.

Disembarking in Cincinnati late the second evening, Brad strolled once around the notorious Fountain Square across from the station and hopped into a red VW beetle. The husky, collegiate, dark-haired driver -- a spitting image of Warren Beatty -- took him home to bed, breakfast, and a little playful bondage and spanking. Residing in a terraced hillside apartment overlooking the city, he turned out to be a popular local disc jockey who didn't need to report to work before noon -- so he ferried Brad out to the edge of town for his final hitch.

Once the prodigal arrived home, all the promises made to him came true -- and then some. He even seduced his bridegroom friend (in the shower before they got dressed for the wedding).

Thanks to Brad's survivalism, his passive attractiveness to more aspiring, stronger guys -- and to plain old luck -- he has led a much happier life than the footloose young man on the pier in Miami might have hoped for. He and Larry visited some, until Larry became lost to drugs and disappeared. A few years later, Brad had far surpassed the domestic status of Skipper and Dale, materially and otherwise. He had converted to monogamy; he has kept only one secret. He's harbored few conscious thoughts of Dave until just the other day, more than thirty years after they met at Frenchie's. Between planes in Chicago, Brad impulsively searched the huge phone book and found his old accomplice's name and studio address in bold black letters... (or surely, wasn't he *Dave's* accomplice?) No matter, luck had favored them both: neither has repented or gone crazy, as movies and soap operas would have it. He put down the phone.

Most nights Brad sleeps fairly well, nestled against his longtime lover. But now and then he does awaken, still leery of God, and nauseous from the same fitful dream of old Southern houses, Bette Davis, sticky foreplay in a darkened balcony, and the sudden opening of a car trunk.

* * *

ABOUT THE AUTHOR

STEVE DUNHAM is a native Ohioan, an alumnus of Kenyon College and Northwestern University, and was for 18 years a journalist, editor, and publicist. Favorite highlights of his reporting career include the Detroit Riot and interviewing Andy Warhol. His fiction has appeared in Genre Magazine.

Author of other stories and a one-act play about friendships dissolved by AIDS, he is a traveler, art collector, and resident of Skidaway Island, Georgia.

CPSIA information can be obtained
at www.ICGtesting.com
Printed in the USA
BVHW072220040122
625216BV00002B/231